TANGLED ROOTS

TANGLED MAGIC SERIES: BOOK ONE

DENISE D. YOUNG

I0626449

Sage & Shadows Books

Text copyright © 2019 by Denise D. Young.
Published by Sage & Shadows Books.

eISBN: 978-0-9980756-2-4
print ISBN: 978-0-9980756-3-1

Cover Design: Victoria Cooper Art
Developmental Editing: Susan Bischoff, The Forge Book Finishers
Proofreading: Maple Cat Press
Formatting: Maple Cat Press

TANGLED
ROOTS

PROLOGUE

Willow Creek, Virginia, 1974

Cassie

There was wildness in the air.

I tipped my head back, breathing it in. The languid summer heat hit my bare throat.

Mine, the magic whispered.

Yes, my soul whispered back. *Yes, all things wild and sacred, all things born of the goddess's womb.*

Yes.

Long blond hair fell across my face. I untied the swath of white ribbon fastened at my throat and secured it in a loose ponytail at my nape.

My hand shook as I withdrew it, damp with moisture from the back of my neck.

It was the summer heat, I reasoned. Nothing more.

Not Nathan's letter, not the memory of his harsh, accusatory voice.

Not the dreams that followed, the fear that I'd turn a corner or open a door and see my hulking brother's form looming over me.

Not the words he'd written that were seared into my brain—words that others might take as a plea but I knew to be a command.

Come home.

The tremors raked my body again, an old fear of magic caged.

Willow Creek was home. My coven was home. Buttercup Diner, where I waited tables and wiped greasy hands on my red apron, that was home.

That little white house in the Georgia mountains, where I could look at the forest but never enter it? That attic bedroom where magic stalked inside my soul like a carnival's caged lion, muscles primed but never able to pounce, aching for release?

That was not home.

I'd watched the Summer of Love and Woodstock come and go. I'd watched both the upheaval and freedom. But I'd been a bystander. In this world. In my life.

I wasn't anymore.

Nathan would make me one again.

My breath quickened.

I didn't know how my brother found me—didn't care. I hadn't thought he or my parents cared enough to look. But I knew Nathan was on a mission from Mama, and that meant soon enough he'd be pounding at my door.

I smoothed my damp palm across the cotton fabric of my knee-length eyelet dress—handmade. Continuing to make my clothes by hand was one of the few remnants of home I allowed myself. The whir of the sewing machine, its rhythm a reassuring beat. The tug of needle and thread until my fingers bled.

Good discipline, my father said.

Keeps her mind off things, Mama always agreed.

Just because the world's gone to hell in a handbasket doesn't mean you have to.

Nathan's words, pounding in my head. I had burnt the letter before one of my coven sisters could see it. I spoke words of release, trying to free myself from the past.

It wasn't enough.

I could feel the blood that connected us, pulling me toward him—toward my past.

And from my fear, this spell emerged.

If I dug deep enough in my magic, I could summon the Guardian of Willow Creek, Virginia. She could block Nathan's path.

She could stop him from dragging me back to that place where I was barely half-alive.

I exhaled, the sound almost sharp in the sleepy forest, the way a drop of water in a cave is magnified.

Ginny, my high priestess, my mentor, was back at the farmhouse she called home, a scant half-mile hike across wooded hills and neatly tended rows of crops. She'd been at her sketchpad when I left her house, her blond hair in a careless braid as she drew the pattern for her next quilt.

Her eyes locked with mine for a split second, a glint of caution in them. "Be careful."

I'd felt her gaze on me as the screen door squeaked shut behind me.

I felt it still, the magic of the coven a thread gently tugging on my own magic.

I pressed my palms to rich, dark soil. I knelt against the forest floor, not caring about the stains on my dress.

Inhale. Balmy summer night, scent of sunbaked earth

and Virginia pine.

Exhale. *Release the past.*

Open my eyes. *Look forward.*

I struck a match, my hand's tremble lessened now, but still there. The scent of freshly struck sulfur stung my nostrils. Upon the matchhead danced a wisp of a magical creature, its body living flame—a salamander, an elemental of fire.

I pressed the match to the waiting black votive candle made by one of my coven sisters, Tricia, and watched as the flame took root on the wick. The salamander stretched out tiny arms, dancing—beauty, magic, fire personified.

"Bless this space, element of fire," I whispered to her.

I took up a feather, one I found shortly after the summer solstice. Ginny had told me it was from a barred owl. "The barred owl is a familiar of the Guardian," Ginny remarked. "She's got a close eye on you." Serious, those words—and her tone a little curious.

I moved the feather up, down, diagonal, forming the shape of a pentacle in the air.

"Bless this space, element of air." I felt, not saw, the moment the sylph arrived—for air was my element, my magic. A witch could work with any elemental magic, of course, but she—or he—always had a close affinity for one. Air was mine.

The sylph hovered behind me, the beat of her wings stirring the air, but she didn't show herself. "Caution, lovely witch. There are silver wisps of magic stirring around you this night. What you work brings deep change. Tread lightly."

Magic tingled across my skin like falling glitter, and then I felt her retreat.

Riddles. Elementals, when they spoke at all to mere mortals, always spoke in riddles.

Next, I took out a small mason jar and poured the water in a slow circle around the lit candle, careful not to disturb the flame, though the salamander within had vanished back to her realm. The water was from Willow Creek, which formed the westernmost boundary of Ginny's farm, and for which the town itself was named.

"Bless this space, element of water."

None of the undine appeared, and I didn't expect them to, though sometimes I heard a hint of their song drifting on the air. But only silence reached my ears this night.

I shook away the sense of foreboding. It was only the rising magic, I reasoned, that made the temperature seem to drop. It was only my lingering concern over Nathan's letter that made my stomach queasy.

Without looking, I reached into the familiar wicker basket and withdrew the last item—the most important.

Earth.

The Guardian of Willow Creek was, at her heart, a being of earth. That much I knew, though I knew little else about her—save that she was powerful, temperamental, and did not suffer fools.

Was I such a fool?

Ginny's warnings about the Guardian almost stilled my hand, but I clutched the bag of silvery-green moss harder. There was no going back. Not now, after two years of freedom. I'd run from home the night of my high school graduation, buying a bus ticket to New York City with money saved up from some sewing jobs I'd done for Mama's friends.

New York City, I'd figured, was as far away from that little farmhouse as I could get. It was a big enough place to vanish into the crowds. And in that anonymity, I'd reasoned, I could find freedom.

Turned out, I found it in this small Virginia town instead. And I'd risk the Guardian's wrath before I'd risk being dragged backward.

I carefully encircled the black votive with the moss, pressing it against the waiting earth. Tendrils of magic snaked into the earth, in hues of amber brown and leafy green.

"Bless this space, element of earth."

"A witch in time saves nine."

I smirked slightly at the gnome's garbled rendition of the familiar phrase. "A *stitch* in time saves nine," I corrected.

"Not this time." There was a gentle rustle, and I felt the elementals, having blessed the space, all retreat.

Inhale.

The scent of earth was heavy now, even for the forest. Maidenhair fern's spice. Mushroom's pungent aroma. Damp stone's musty scent.

The ground underneath me seemed to tilt and sway.

I rose on unsteady feet. An unseen force slammed me into the tree behind me. I crumpled against the thick trunk, stars dancing in my vision.

The candle went out. I fell, though I was already lying on the forest floor. The ground gave way, and I fell.

⚜

Torch flames danced. Quartz crystal points in their many forms—clear as glass, smoky gray, the yellow of citrine, the purple of amethyst, and pale pink of rose quartz—jutted from the earth below and cavernous ceiling above. Silver moss dangled. The eyes of unseen creatures peered from the shadows, hidden by swirling silvery mists.

The mists before me parted, revealing a throne carved of dark, twisting wood, as though the tree from which it was carved were still alive, still sentient, still growing. Green crystals poked out here and there. Behind it was a wall of dark green vines speckled with red roses the size of small cabbages.

But it was the figure who sat in that throne—and such a chair could only rightly be called a throne—who sent my jaw dropping.

"Cassandra Anne Gearhart." Full lips, a deep, plum purple, almost black, but glistening as though they'd kissed the stars, turned upward in a dark, sinister smile as they hissed my name.

I stepped backward, but a wall of vines pressed against me, halting any retreat. "Yes?"

Her eyes were silver like the mists, but bright as the coldest of winter stars. Her skin was bronze as though stained with earth, her hair a twisting mass of light brown braids filled with moss and twigs.

She rose. I was short—a mere five-foot—so most people seemed tall to me, but she was purely a giantess. She towered over me, her robes the same near-black purple as her lips, threaded with green, amber, and teal threads. I almost reached out to caress the billowing fabric, to test its fibers under my fingers. Instead, I curled my fingers into my palms.

She reached out with bony fingers and tilted my head upwards until I strained to meet her glinting gaze.

That smile again. Wise and wicked. "I will grant your wish."

"You'll…" I sucked in my lips. It was too easy. I shouldn't have done this. "You'll make sure Nathan can't find me."

She nodded, each bob of her head deliberate, decisive. "Yes. But there's a price."

"What would you ask of me?" The words came out a little too high, too desperate. Never a good position when one was facing such a powerful being.

"I see far more than you, and I am not obligated to tell you all that I see," she snapped.

I lowered my gaze back to the wall of vines. "Of course, my lady."

She released my chin from her bony clutches, and I sighed with relief. "One day, you will awaken. You will sleep for many years, and, when I need you, you will awaken."

"I don't understand. How does that stop…How does that grant my wish?"

A gust of wind shook the cavern. "I do *not* owe little mortals explanations." She tilted her head, as if listen to whispers the wind carried. "He's here, you know. Your father is sick. Do you want to go home?"

"I want to stay in Willow Creek."

"Then you'll stay. I can make that so. Do you agree to my terms?"

"I don't understand your terms." I inhaled, wishing I could suck the words back in, swallow them.

To my surprise, she chuckled. "You don't need to. If I release you this night without granting your wish, he will find you. Or you can accept my offer. But I'm not a creature of patience, immortal though I might be."

That attic bedroom. Those woods I couldn't enter. What fate could be worse than magic caged?

"I accept."

She nodded. "Then as I will it, so mote it be."

Ribbons of magic twisted in the air, wrapping around me, tugging me back up through the earth.

"I know she's here, bitch!"

My blood ran cold at those words. I tried to crane my

head, to see where Nathan's voice had come from, but every muscle was stiff, frozen.

"Don't you dare speak to me that way. Get off my land. This is private property." Ginny's voice, madder than I'd ever heard her.

Nathan came into view. He'd grown a beard since last I'd last seen him, and even in the moonlight I could see how red his face was. "Where is she? Cassandra? Cassie!"

I'd seen my brother angry before and, not for the first time, I feared that in his rage he'd hurt me. I tried to run, but my feet were rooted to the earth.

He glared down at the candle, pointing at the now extinguished flame. The spell was over, the magic cast.

What had I done wrong? Why hadn't she saved me?

Why couldn't I run?

Ginny got in Nathan's path, blocking him. She was tall for a woman and matched his height. "Boy, unless you want an ass full of birdshot, get off my farm. Do you hear me?"

Nathan strode off into the woods, calling my name. Why hadn't he seen me? I was standing right in front of him.

The tension in me eased as he stomped off, the sound of him yelling my name growing more distant.

Ginny knelt down and picked up a handful of moss and the owl feather. She shifted them from palm to palm, as if testing the weight of the spell's remnants in her hands. "Cassie. Miss Cassie, what have you gone and done?"

She gasped. Her eyes flew open, the moss tumbling down, the feather fluttering toward the ground. She spun to face me. She reached out and raked her hands against my cheek, but her touch was distant, as though through layer upon layer of papier-mâché. "Oh, child, sweet Cassie. Why has she done this to you?"

I tried to speak, to ask her what she meant. I tried to

shift my weight, to meet her gaze. Nothing. I was rooted.

Then I realized—I was, indeed, rooted in the earth.

A tree. The Guardian had made me a tree.

I tried to open my mouth to scream.

All those years, my magic trapped inside, and now, again, in my haste to maintain freedom, I was trapped.

"Shush, child." As though she felt my pain, Ginny smiled a comforting smile. She sat on the forest floor, cupping the candle in her palm, and began to sing.

"Where the undine sings her sweet, wild song,
I met my beloved there.
Where the willow drapes her green, green hair,
I met my beloved there.
Where water flows over tumbled stone,
Where magic meets the earth,
Where the willow drapes her green, green hair,
I met my beloved there."

Long after her voice grew hoarse, she sang. They weren't songs I'd ever heard before—not as we shelled peas, sipped sweet tea, or chatted long into the night on her porch, nor as the coven sisters gathered and worked magic under the moon. Perhaps, she wrote them this night, lyrics plucked from the ether just for me.

Eventually, my heart grew light, enveloped in song like a sleepy child wrapped in a downy comforter. Somehow, the magic of her simple melodies was like a draught of peace.

I slept.

And slept.

And slept.

CHAPTER ONE

Willow Creek, Virginia, 2019

Nick

The scent of rain hung heavy on the air. I leaned against the porch rail and took another swig of my iced tea. Though I'd worked since the morning on the farm, the tension in my neck wasn't from hard labor. I was twenty-three, and still had plenty of years before farm work would leave me with arthritis like Gran. It wasn't my body that feared the rain, the thunder, the lightning's jagged tongue.

It was my heart that was sick, my heart that remembered. Broken.

That was me, Nick Felson, the only witch the torrent left behind.

Bile rose bitter in my throat.

That's why I was leaving, going somewhere no one knew who the hell I was.

The harvest for tomorrow's farmers' market was

already picked and stored in the barn to protect it from the gathering rain. Soon enough, this place wouldn't be my problem anymore.

This place. Home.

It was a weight too heavy to bear alone. Not the work—the memories.

Gravel crunched under car tires, and I turned to see a silver sedan, sparkling and new, pulling into the driveway.

The driver's door opened, and a foot clad in a stiletto heel popped out. Mary Jo Grayson, a perky sixty-something with a slender physique and chin-length gray hair emerged, her precariously thin heels seeking purchase on the gravel.

I set my glass beside the porch rail and jogged over, offering an arm. Mom and Gran had worked hard to teach me manners, after all.

"Thanks, Nicholas," she said with a breathy laugh.

"Thanks for coming, Mrs. Grayson," I said, echoing her formality.

Once on the more even flagstone pathway leading to the house, she stepped back and stared up at the yellow farmhouse. It wasn't much. Peeling yellow paint needed to be scraped and repainted. And the house, built in 1920, had been generously sized at the time but was small by modern standards.

But it wasn't the house that made Saunders Farm such a prime catch. No, it was the land. Surely there was someone out there who hadn't heard about what had happened here that night last year, some developer who wouldn't care about the whispers of tragedy that lived here.

Mary Jo adjusted the strap of her red leather tote bag over her shoulder. "Why don't you show me around?"

I managed to mumble a response. Folks were used to

me mumbling. My brother, Evan, got all the charisma and swagger. *"You're serious, like your granddaddy was,"* Mom always said. I never met him—he died in Vietnam when Mom was a baby.

My breath caught, but I'd learned to calm myself so I didn't make a spectacle. I'd never had a panic attack a day in my life until that night.

I led her into the house, trying to do what the article I'd read online said and talk up the small farmhouse's features. "Up-to-date kitchen, original woodwork, lots of natural light…"

Mary Jo nodded, occasionally jotting something down on a yellow legal pad, her voice bubbly and effusive with praise over the house.

Far across the Virginia mountains, thunder rumbled.

There's magic in these hills, Nick. Gran's words, rich with a country accent that flowed like raw clover honey, echoed in my mind.

And her eyes, blue like my own, were there also.

I can't, Gran. I just can't anymore.

Mary Jo sat at the table, flipping through some documents she'd pulled out of her tote bag with its shiny gold logo. "So, I'm curious, what made you decide to sell?"

The phrase, "after all this time" hung unspoken, like a wisp of smoke curling in the air.

I swallowed, ignoring the first splash of rain against the earth. "I got an offer for a job from a friend of mine out in Arizona."

"Oh." Mary Jo raised an eyebrow. Small town downfall. Everybody knew—or wanted to know—everybody's business.

"Yeah." I shoved my hands into the pockets of my battered Levi's. Soon enough, I'd be covered in desert dust, watching tumbleweeds and photographing grip-and-grin photos featuring ribbon-cuttings of playgrounds and hair salons for a struggling newspaper. It wasn't anybody's dream job. It was just...not here.

"What kind of work?"

I sighed. *Give people the bare minimum. Just enough to shut them up but not so much that everybody knows everything.* "Newspaper photographer." It was for a small-town paper—population 5,000. The work was only part-time, but it was a place to start to get my life back on track. And I could live off the money from the sale of the farm while I tried to start fresh, away from a place where everybody had their own version of what happened that night, and away from where the girls I dated touched my hand in pity.

Mary Jo nodded. "Good for you. That's what you were studying in college, if I recall. And weren't you interning at the Morning Glory Gazette, before—" She clamped her mouth shut over the words, her eyes widening. She shook her head, fumbling for a pen in her impossibly large bag. "Just sign here. This is just a document saying you've authorized me to represent you in the sale of the property. I'll pull some comps and we'll come up with a decent listing price." The words were a little more compressed than before. Nervous.

That didn't take long.

I took the pen she offered, saying nothing about her near slipup.

Lightning flashed. The pen tumbled out of my hand, skittering across the oak farmhouse table and onto the hardwood. Wordlessly, I scooped it back up and scrawled a sloppier-than-usual signature across the bottom of the page.

"All set." Mary Jo tapped the papers against the table and slid them into a manila folder, her smile a little too kind, as though she'd softened it just for a poor soul like me—a twenty-three-year-old man afraid of a little thunder. "I'll be in touch soon. The market's strong right now. Shouldn't take long to sell a property like this one."

She reached the back door, her hand on the knob.

"Do you want to wait out the storm?" Damn, but even I heard the desperate quiver in my voice.

"No. I'll stay safe." She met my gaze, hers softening. Again, that damned pity. "Don't worry. I'll swing by soon with the comps."

As the back door closed, the scent of the storm wafted in, along with another scent. Damp soil. Bonfire. Candle wax.

The scent of magic.

But it couldn't be. Because no one had worked magic on this farm in almost a year.

Mary Jo walked carefully through the rain-splattered gravel and climbed into her sedan. I stared transfixed at her taillights as she drove away in the dim light of the storm. Only after they'd vanished did I realize I should've walked her to her car.

Thunder cracked, promising a long night ahead.

And the scent of magic lingered. I rubbed my neck, where fine filaments of hair prickled, my own magic stirring in response. I gritted my teeth and tamped it back down.

To distract myself, I turned on the TV, some dumb reality show, anything to drown out the sound of the storm.

In my head, I repeated my mantra, the words that kept me sane for eleven—now almost twelve—months.

You can go the rest of your life without doing magic.

❧

Cassie

My thirsty roots drank up the water from the earth, and I sighed. Though it had been indefinably long since I'd been muscle and sinew, I imagined my body resting heavily against a mattress as the storm sang to me a rock-and-roll lullaby.

As I had so many times throughout the years, I drifted away from my oak-bound body, back toward another time. I was fifteen again, trapped in a very different way.

I sighed, falling back into my past in a way that came so easily in this form.

The wind, my first love, had rapped its knuckles against my window like a lover. I'd thrown off the covers and pushed open the window, shoving the rusty sash hard, hoping my dad didn't hear over the storm.

Wind, with his wildness, rushed in. The *Love Bug* poster on my wall threatened to tear from its thumbtack moorings. I tilted my head. I gasped at the feel of those rough, yet airy fingers in my hair, knowing the way I'd emerge tangled and red-faced from his embrace.

My body shook with the thunder, the spray of summer rain against my face washing away the traces of sleep. A storm of magic built within me, the release building. I closed my eyes as the wind caressed me—air magic, wild and pure.

Rough fingers had grasped my wrist. My eyes flew open, lids like birds startled into flight.

Nathan.

His blond hair was cropped short, his blue eyes twin storms of fury. "Stop. You think I can't feel what you're doing? Stop working magic." His words were a low growl—even he daren't wake our parents. Eighteen years old, and full of anger.

I tugged my wrist away, the magic retreating. The storm grew distant.

Nathan towered over me, an impossible hulk. He always seemed to grow, and I never seemed to.

He turned away and shut the window, the rusted latch closing with a reluctant groan.

"Go to bed," he hissed over his shoulder. I caught a strong odor on his breath—his secret stash of whiskey, again? At the doorway, he paused, and even in the stormy shadows I saw the silhouette of his body trembling. "You'll curse us all," he whispered, the words raw and ragged, barely audible above the storm.

A blinding crack, like the sound of a rifle being discharged, shook the forest. There was no time to mistake it for thunder. A pain gripped me in a sharp-clawed hand, jerking me back to the present day.

Back to Willow Creek, and the forest of freedom that had become my prison.

The oak splintered, like bones breaking. My new body gave a terrible groan as it toppled.

❋

Cassie

My eyes, still clouded with deep sleep, fluttered open. The kiss of rain lingered against my skin, now cool on the summer night. Clouds hung heavy in the night sky, remnants of a storm recently passed. I sat up, my head pounding, and swiped my hands uselessly at leaves and dirt clinging to my damp skin.

The scent of magic hung in the electrically charged air—bonfire's woodsmoke and melting candle wax mingled with the scent of fresh rain.

This was...different. The last I remembered, I'd come to the woods to work a spell. The storm? The outcome of the spell? Nothing.

I stood gingerly, staggering to the side.

The trunk of a fallen oak caught me. Freshly fallen, by the look of its still-green leaves. A charred stench lingered on the air.

This wasn't right.

What happened?

A cloud drifted away from the half-moon. Hadn't it been newly nearly full earlier tonight?

Ginny. If anyone had answers, she would.

My bare feet dug into damp soil, searching for purchase as I made my way across the fields toward the yellow farmhouse where Ginny always waited with a hot cup of tea and words of wisdom.

Every inch of me was soaked—long hair dripping, my eyelet dress stained and plastered to my skin. Shivers raked me as I stumbled through the soggy fields toward the promise of sanctuary that yellow house represented.

Aching, I climbed up the back-porch steps and leaned against the railing.

With a gasp, I tugged on the screen door, only to find it locked. Strange. Ginny never locked the back door. Sisters were free to come and go as they pleased.

Nathan. The memory of watching my brother's letter burn in my kitchen sink washed over me. Was he looking for me? Had he been here?

I knocked against the back door harder than necessary.

"Please, please." I didn't know who I was talking to. I

just wanted Ginny's tall, lanky figure to fill the doorway. I banged again, the door rattling under the force of my knuckles.

The porch light flickered to life, and I blinked in the painful brightness. The door swung open.

"Can I help you?" an irritated male voice asked.

I stepped back, but it wasn't my brother who filled the doorway. A man, scarcely a few years my senior, with familiar blue eyes set in a scruffy, hardened face, stared down at me.

His gaze was hard, and I let mine fall to his arms, to the kind of biceps a man earned through hour after hour of manual labor. I swallowed. "Who...?"

"Do you know what time it is?" he snapped.

I laughed, a slightly panicked edge to the sound. "I can honestly say I haven't a clue."

"Well, just spit out what you want. Your car break down? Cell service is spotty out here."

"What?" I leaned into the slight dash of comfort I got from the familiar Virginia drawl in his words—though I didn't understand about half of them.

"Do you need to call someone?" he asked slowly, as though I were dumb.

I struggled, found my tongue. "I'm looking for Ginny."

His tan face paled. His broad hands formed white-knuckled fists at his sides. "She's dead."

I stumbled backwards until my back hit the porch rail. I fumbled for it, but missed, hitting the worn porch wood with a sharp thud.

The man cursed and flung the screen door open. He knelt beside me, examining my eyes. "Have you been drinking?" he asked, clearly more than a little irritated.

I swallowed, my throat dry. "I don't...drink." I pressed

my palm to my forehead. "I don't…she was just here. Was it Nathan? Did Nathan do this?" What would he do to my high priestess in one of his rages?

"Ginny's been dead for a year." He glared at me. "Who's Nathan?"

"My…" I started to answer, but his words hit me like a bus. I stumbled to my feet, leaning against the rail. "A year? No. Just yesterday. I…What?"

He turned from me and raked hands through hair a little too shaggy.

I waited, my body tense, the shivers now not just from the chill.

After a minute, he spun back to face me. He seemed to work at softening his face. "You knew her?"

Pain etched his words. I nodded, unable to find any of my own.

"You can come inside and call someone, and then you need to be on your way. Understood?"

He didn't wait for my answer, just stepped back into the house and held the door open.

Inside that little old farmhouse was sanctuary—hand-sewn quilts, loose-leaf tea, chipped teacups, and walls reverberating with the laughter of gathered coven sisters.

I stepped over the threshold, but the energy of the house was changed. Whatever this was, it wasn't the Willow Creek I remembered.

CHAPTER TWO

Nick

Magic. She stunk of it. My throat vibrated with a near-silent growl.

Gods damn it all.

Not sure who she thought she was, knocking on my door at midnight, silvery-blue air magic swirling in her aura.

I yanked a quilt from the chest in the living room and unfurled one of my grandmother's creations to wrap around my shivering houseguest. This one was a log cabin design in simple red and cream. The scent of cedar and lavender sachets drifted up from the worn cotton. Hell, my guest was covered in dirt, as though she'd slept in the woods, but that would wash off. Gran always said her quilts weren't meant for show; they were meant for real life.

Apparently, this was it.

I stomped back into the kitchen, worn hardwood meeting the heavy footfalls of my bare feet. My head felt full of cotton, a sign of an oncoming panic attack.

I held out the quilt, trying not to notice the startled way my guest gawked at me, her mouth agape as she perched on the edge of a chair, like she wasn't sure whether or where to bolt.

I swallowed. "Tea?" The word came out a strange croak. I cleared my throat. "Tea. Do you want some?"

She smiled. "Yes." I busied my shaking hand filling the kettle.

"We don't filter," I rambled, wincing at the posthumous *we*. "I have the well water tested yearly, and the taste is better than anything you'll find bottled in the grocery store."

She laughed, a little high, as if taut with nerves, but also with a hint of merriment. "What?"

I waited for the pilot light on the propane stove to click, then set the kettle on the burner. I watched the steady blue flame beneath the blue kettle, not wanting to turn to my impromptu houseguest, hating the warring emotions.

I tried not to hear or to feel other witches' magic—on the rare occasions I encountered them. But this woman's...

I sighed. The air hummed with it. She was the promise of the summer stars, the crackle of a bonfire, the brush of a feather against bare skin, the scent wafting from a field of lavender.

No. No. A thousand times no.

I spun and placed my palms against the kitchen island, keeping my distance. Mostly for myself, but she also seemed startled, shocked, and beyond confused. No need to loom over her with that "brooding farm boy thing" that Evan always told me to play up. "Girls like that," he'd said.

Maybe for a fling—which, thankfully, was all I ever offered.

I caught her studying me, a quizzical expression on her face. "Folks buy water in stores?"

"Yeah..."

She sucked in her lips and shook her head. "I'm sorry. It's been the longest night of my life... in many ways." Her tone was careful and clipped, almost forced cheer, but I heard sorrow.

And then I understood. "You knew my grandmother?"

She nodded, wrapped the quilt tighter around her body, and peered out the bay window into the darkness. "She was my mentor."

"She never mentioned having a student outside the coven." I shifted. Gran often kept her opinions to herself, and she didn't share coven business outside the coven. She respected people's privacy. I'd barely even heard her gossip—and everyone in Willow Creek gossiped. Even the men. "I'm Nick, by the way. Ginny's grandson."

She laughed, the sound bordering on hysterical. "I'm sorry. Maeve is just a child."

I shook my head. This woman was out of her mind. "No. Mom is—was—the local midwife."

She stared at me like I was a ghost—in my own home. "What year is it?"

"Umm..." Gods, but she'd worked one wild spell out in those woods if she was this confused. "2019."

Her legs wobbled, and I barely caught her before helping her into one of the kitchen chairs. "And you're Nick. Maeve's son. Ginny's grandson."

"That's me. Nick Felson." I exhaled. It was a relief, somehow, the first time in forever I'd met someone who didn't know who I was, who didn't have their own version of what happened by the banks of Willow Creek on Saunders Family Farm. Although, whether she was sane? That had yet to be determined.

She nodded. "That was Ginny's father's name, wasn't

it? Nicholas?"

"Yeah. It was." That wasn't exactly a secret. Anyone with Internet access could find that information. "And you are?"

She stood, her legs still shaky, but she seemed full of frenetic energy. I couldn't help noticing the way she began to move around the kitchen—with familiar ease, as though she was a frequent guest. "Cassie. Cassie Gearhart."

"Cassie." Her name slipped off my tongue, tasting of summer—of dandelion salad, mint iced tea, a tiny drop of sweet honeysuckle.

My sleeping magic threatened to surface. The scent of a freshly ploughed field rose up, along with a hint of mushrooms, a wild forest of fir and pine.

She tilted her head. "You inherited your grandmother's gifts."

"They're not a gift," I snapped.

She raised an eyebrow. "I know some people think that, but you can't—"

"I'm not discussing this with a stranger." Her fingers were worrying the wood of the farmhouse table, tracing the pattern of the grains. "Who sent you here? I told them months ago to stay away."

Her brow furrowed. "Told who?"

"The other covens. I know they want answers. I'm not their man. You understand?"

She shook her head. The quilt fell away from her shoulders, revealing a stained, previously white sundress that skimmed sun-bronzed thighs. The dress had a vintage vibe, as though she'd plucked it off the rack at a second-hand clothing store.

She reached out, tentative, and touched my arm. "Nick, no one sent me, okay? I'm just…lost. I'm so lost, and really far from home."

"I thought Ginny was your mentor. Were you emailing or something?"

"It's like you're speaking another language half the time. Look, the truth is, when I say I'm not from around here, I don't mean Willow Creek. I mean, now."

"Now? Are you playing freaking mind games? Is that your style? Gaslight the last witch in Willow Creek?"

Before she could respond, the kettle whistled. I jumped back, grunting as I slammed my hip into the corner of the island. With a growl, I turned to the tea kettle. I pulled down two blue pottery mugs emblazoned with pale moons over emerald green mountains. I plucked two tea bags out of a metal canister, not even bothering to check what blend, and set her mug in front of her.

"Honey and sugar are on the island." I inclined my head in that direction.

"I'm confused." She wrapped one hand around the mug and, without asking, opened a drawer and withdrew a spoon. Again, like she'd been here before. Not once, but many times. "Am I staying for tea, or do you want to run me off the property?" She jutted out her chin, and I caught a glimpse of stubborn pride underneath a veil of polite acquiescence.

I scratched the stubble on my chin. "Tell me the truth. Who you are. Why you're here. No games."

"No games."

The words, a mere whisper, tingled in the air with a magical sort of promise. Somehow, without knowing how I knew, whatever she said next would be the truth.

"I cast a spell—to keep my brother away. He was looking for me. To stop me from doing magic. I went out into the woods—with Ginny's, your grandmother's—permission. She was always good about letting me cast spells whenever the mood struck. I'd gone so long." She swallowed and tilted her head back.

Again, I leaned in, drawn by the hint of lavender on the air. I'd never glimpsed another witch's magic this easily. Goddess, but that scared the daylights out of me. Her eyes locked with mine. Somehow, without realizing, I'd bridged the distance between us, until only inches separated us.

"I'd gone so long without doing magic, so she'd let me come here, to make up for lost time."

Wildness stirred in the air. I felt it the way only a witch could feel it—nerve endings electrified, body not sure whether it wanted to stiffen and arch, or melt into the floor.

"Nick." My name left her lips, sizzling with a humid ache.

"Cassie." Gods. It was like I'd said it a million times before, like I would say it a million more before my last breath.

Somehow—gods knew how—she was in my arms. I brushed my fingers against the wild tangle of her hair, a swirl of long, knotted blond mixed with leaves and dirt. "Were you…sleeping in the woods?" The words were heavy, painful.

"I'm not from here."

"You said that." I needed to kiss her. What was wrong with me?

She smiled, almost wistful. "I'm from 1974. I cast a spell…in July of 1974. And I woke up in 2019."

The spell broke, like a bubble popping against my skin. I jerked back. "That's not possible. There are a lot of things possible in this world—a lot more than most folks even dream of. But time travel? That's not one of them."

※

Cassie

He almost kissed me.

I almost let him.

My fingers brushed my lips, still half-hungry. Whatever energy had sizzled in the air between us, it was brand-new to me. The magic I knew was wild and powerful. It could move mountains. But this had been a throbbing beat unlike any I'd ever known. I wasn't sure whether such magic intended to make my soul soar or shatter.

I grasped the edge of the island, still shaky, though the energy had vanished as quickly as it had appeared.

Nick had his back to me, his fingers clutching the edge of the sink. Heat pooled in my belly.

"I'm sorry."

"For what? Time-traveling?" His voice was raw and gritty, full of unspoken pain. I felt it like a knife—as though the wound left in him was also left in me.

"No, for…" I shifted. The fog of confusion lifted long enough for me to see what a spectacle I was making of myself. "I'm not a loose woman, that's all. I don't bang on strangers' doors at all hours of the night and seduce them."

He laughed bitterly. "No, I didn't think you did."

I bristled. I'd never met a male witch before. I knew they existed, but Ginny's coven had been all women during my two years as a member. "Are you making fun of me?"

He shook his head, but didn't turn to face me. "No."

I saw myself through his eyes, then. A foolish girl, lost in time, wearing a ruined handmade dress, in a state of disarray.

And he hated magic. Not the way my parents and my brother hated it—they simply didn't understand it, didn't feel it. No, I didn't know how Nick could feel magic the way I felt it and turn his back on it.

"I'm messing up your night. I'll leave you alone."

Summoning what little grace I could muster, I marched out the backdoor. To go where, I didn't know. I wasn't even wearing shoes.

I was down the steps when I heard the creak of the screen door. "At least let me drive you somewhere."

"No thanks. I'll hitch a ride."

"No. It's not safe." He cleared his throat. "Look, if you are telling the truth, you should know things are different."

I shot him a look over my shoulder. "I *am* telling the truth. But I'll figure things out. I spent most of my life locked in a bedroom when I wasn't at school. I made a life for myself back then. I'll do it again."

My heart was pounding, and I didn't even know why. Anger? Fear? Something else? I couldn't explain this rush of feelings. Was I floating or falling, coming or going, burning in the sweet flames, or drenched in the summer rain? I needed space—and he sounded like he needed it more than I did.

"Have a nice night. Thanks for your help."

I felt the pressure of his gaze against my back long after the shadows of night swallowed me. Gravel bit into my bare feet, but I kept going. There was a little motel out near the highway. I might be able to barter a room for housekeeping services. Folks in town had always been willing to work with each other on things like that.

Please, Goddess, I prayed as I reached the road and began the long trek toward town. *Don't let that much have changed.*

CHAPTER THREE

Nick

I spun around, her image seared into my mind. The damned racing of my heart had nothing to do with panic or bad memories.

What the hell was *that*?

Gran's quilt lay crumpled on the floor. I picked it up, inhaling the familiar scent.

Something fell out of the folds of fabric and clattered to the floor—an earthy green stone. I picked it up, tested its weight in my palm.

Gran's voice drifted toward me, across time, across the ether. I was eight years old again. Mom was working late at the hospital, where she was a nurse-midwife. Evan and I were snuggled into the soft bed in Mom's old room, underneath one of Gran's quilts—navy blue, a pattern of stars.

I don't want to sleep. Evan's voice, always insistence with a healthy dose of charm.

Gran was the only woman on the planet who was

immune. *Sleep, my love.* She soothed back his blond hair, always too long and uneven because he couldn't sit still long enough to let Mom cut it properly. *In dreams, adventures await. There's magic in the dreamworld, too. Sometimes more than in the waking.*

And then her gaze drifted away from Evan, landing softly on me. She kissed my head and leaned toward my ear, smelling of clothes dried in sunshine. *Hold this, Nicholas.* She only called me Nicholas when it was truly important that I listened, and my little ears perked.

Into my hand she slipped a stone—cool, smooth, full of earth. *Nephrite jade, for when you're low. To protect you, my love, when I cannot. To lift you up, when we cannot comfort you. On the other side of suffering, there is hope.*

When she'd said it, Dad had just left.

He didn't do much anyway, Evan later declared, and everyone agreed. But I'd been a kid, he was my dad, and I'd missed him. I'd carried that stone everywhere until it fell out of my pocket one day in the fields.

Witches know the energy of stones, the way non-magic folks know the telling of a story they've read, or the sound of an old friend's voice. Every stone, even of the same type, vibrates a little differently, whispers in its own unique cadence.

This stone was that stone. No mistaking it.

I clutched it, calming energy washing over me. Grounding me. Drawing me out of my head.

The sound of rain against the tin roof drew me out of the meditative trance of the nephrite.

Cassie.

She was confused and, I knew now, telling the truth. Magic did many things. Magic didn't lie. It was as true as the trees. It hid much, roots and rings and ancient secrets, but it didn't deliberately obfuscate. Instead, it was up to the witch to seek, to listen, to find.

Cassie, for some reason, was here. Gran and Mom had taught me to be a gentleman, though it always came more naturally to Evan. I was awkward, serious, and sometimes I forgot—or remembered too late. Since they'd died and the panic attacks started, I'd only gotten worse.

But even I knew that you didn't let a lost and bewildered young woman wander the streets in the rain.

Hitchhiking.

Crap. She didn't know what was out there. I often focused on magical dangers, but the world was full of twisted souls who didn't need magic to do evil.

I jammed my feet into a pair of sneakers, not caring about socks, and grabbed the keys to the pickup off the hook.

"Goddess, protect her. Bathe her in white light. Watch over her—" I stopped myself in the midst of the protection spell. Magic rose inside of me like a building wave. I tamped it down.

"No." I squeezed my hand around the nephrite stone before tucking it into my pocket.

I locked the back door and hurried down the stairs, head bent against the latest deluge of storm.

"You," I grunted as I slid into the driver's seat and buckled my seatbelt, "can go your whole life without doing magic."

I turned the key in the ignition, the rebuilt engine turning over nicely. The truck bounced down the gravel drive.

I repeated the words.

But I didn't believe them as much as I had only hours before.

❀

Cassie

I gasped as my feet slid in the wet grass at the roadside. I hit the earth, palms first. Gravel bit into my skin, but I pushed myself up with a huff.

Fat plops of rain hit my skin. My hair and dress were still soaked.

Goddess.

How did I end up here, out of my own time?

"To right a wrong, to make a right. To birth the dawn out of year-long night."

I jumped, my hand flying to my throat. My gaze landed on a short, stout figure in the rainy shadows. I knew the sound of a gnome's voice, high and chirpy, yet with a hint of earth's gravel. And the scent of mushrooms and dirt wafted through the air.

"What?"

"You'll see, you'll see. And so it shall be."

He vanished with the sound of a bubble bursting, his body disappearing back below the earth to his subterranean home. Elemental of earth, that one.

Rain fell faster, obscuring my vision even further.

Did anything I remembered still exist? Four and a half decades had passed, if Nick spoke true. Everything I remembered about Willow Creek could've been gone.

I bit my lip. I would not scream.

My coven, my heart-sisters—sisters not in blood, but in magic—were gone. Dead.

An old feeling, long extinguished, rose up like a great, terrifying bird.

"You. Will. Not," I ground through my teeth, spitting

each word out like an angry bit of venom.

Not the old hopelessness. Not the despair.

The rain crashed down, a flash of lightning. My legs no longer had the strength to go on, but I forced them.

"This is who I am," I whispered to the rain. "I am the one who builds anew. Forward. Always forward."

And the past? What of your roots?

A voice inside, but not my own. I'd long experienced what Ginny called clairaudience, an ability to hear voices from the spirit plane. It was rare, but among those who possessed it, almost all were blessed with air magic.

"I am rooted in wind. Birds have no roots."

To be what you are meant to be, you must connect to the ones born of the same roots.

The words hit me like a freight train.

"Never."

I pushed my legs forward.

A car approached behind me, and a swath of headlights cut through the storm's nighttime shadows. The car slowed.

"Cassie."

I turned. "Nick. I didn't think you wanted to see me again."

He sighed. "Just get in. You can stay tonight."

"Maybe you could just give me a ride to town."

He leaned across the seat and popped open the passenger door. I climbed in with a shiver.

"You're a mess."

I glared. "And you, sir, are not a gentleman."

"No. Mom and Gran tried their best, but I guess I turned out a little rough."

There was pain in those words, and I wished I could take mine back.

He shook his head. "Don't know why I said that." I

caught a bit of color rising in his cheeks as the interior light faded in the truck cab.

He slid the shifter into gear. "So? Town? Or the farmhouse?"

"I don't know."

He shifted into park and leaned back. I heard the roughness of his breath, felt his magic trapped, but wanting to dance, like a pinned foot trying to tap to the sounds of a fiddle and drum.

"I don't do magic, okay? That's just it. And no, I'm not giving you an explanation."

"That's okay. You have a right to your privacy, same as everyone else."

"Do I, though? Does anyone in a small town? Don't you ever just want to go somewhere where no one knows who the hell you are or where you've been?"

I snorted. "In a way. My whole life, no one ever saw who I really was. Troubled. That's what everyone called me. I had no friends. The one guy who dated me did it just to see if the rumors were true. My parents feared me. My brother hated me. And then I came here. And there was love. And people saw me for who I really was. I wouldn't trade that for anything."

His sigh had an edge, like broken glass. "That's all gone now."

"There's nothing lost that can't be found again." I automatically echoed Ginny's words. "It takes a different form, but it is still the spirit. And though spirit changes forms, it is unending."

"You did know her."

"And she me." Tears stung my eyes. Ginny, gone. And I had no idea how or why. All of my coven sisters—gone. "Better than anyone ever knew me, ever."

Nick's hand slid across the fabric of the seat. His fingers, hot and slightly damp, grasped mine. "That was her gift."

For a few minutes, we sat there in the silence, two strangers holding hands, adrift in the dark.

The bright glare of headlights broke the spell. A vehicle came toward us and slowed down. A window rolled down in the storm.

"Trouble, Nick?" a man's voice rumbled.

"No, sir. Just heading home now."

The man, mid-seventies, leaned forward and peered into the darkness of the cab. "Got a friend?"

"Someone from out of town."

"Hmm." The man waited, seeming to want more info, then continued on his way.

Nick's exhale was audible. "Well, we'll see where that leads in the morning. Everybody talks here. You know that, right?"

I smiled, but my stomach knotted at the thought of being the subject of gossip. I'd always tried to stay as amiable as possible—and therefore made an unlikely subject for such chatter. Polite, agreeable, sweet, mysterious, Cassie Gearhart. "Yeah. I know."

"You want to go to town?"

Thunder cracked overhead. Nick jumped.

"Hey." I reached for his hand, found it clutched on the steering wheel. "I want to go back to the farm. If there are any answers, that's where they'll be. If your invitation still stands."

"It does."

His hand trembled underneath mine. After a few seconds, he withdrew it to shift once more into drive. He managed a deft three-point turn, and we rumbled back toward the Saunders Family Farm.

Back in the drive, we sprinted through the rain. Nick shut the door behind us.

"Is there any chance I could take a shower?" I asked, smiling sheepishly. "I'm in a bit of a state."

"I'd actually encourage it," he said, returning my smile. He spun away quickly, though, as though he hadn't intended his playfulness. "There are towels on the shelf in the bathroom, and soap and shampoo in the shower. I'll find something for you to wear and set it outside the bathroom door."

He stomped off into the dark hallway.

In the bathroom, all the products seemed local, handmade. A bottle of rosemary-mint shampoo, the label read, was made here in Willow Creek, along with a bar of patchouli-scented soap.

I breathed in as hot water streamed over my skin. Tears threatened to fall, but I had years of practice in bottling up unpleasant emotions.

"Everything is lost," I whispered to the air. I wanted to believe, but the strangeness swept over me. Some things—like the scent of homemade soap—were so familiar, and yet other things so strange.

Not lost forever. Just waiting to be found. That voice, a woman's, deep and ancient as the mountains.

I twisted the brass knobs, stopping the flow of hot water, and stepped out of the steamy shower, wrapping my body in a green towel.

"In a new way." Wasn't that the promise? I closed my eyes, opened them, then busied myself wiping the mirror free of fog with my hand. "But what does that mean?"

CHAPTER FOUR

Nick

Cassie snored. My lips lifted in a rare smile, and the softness of the muscle movement felt strange. Guess I didn't use those muscles much these days.

I spooned coffee into the coffee press—a dark roast with a hint of cocoa from Mad Moon Roastery. Yeah, they were two hippies who lived in a tiny house and had a roastery in town. But that was the flavor of Willow Creek—equal parts quirky small businesses, bluegrass music, and Southern small-town folks who knew everything about everybody.

Crap. Pete McCafferty saw Cassie in my truck last night, just sitting in the middle of the road. Pete wasn't much of a talker, but his wife, Lucy, was. And no doubt Mary Jo had told plenty of people about me leaving town. Who knew what questions folks would be asking at the farmers' market today?

I shut off the kettle just before it began to whistle so the sound wouldn't wake Cassie. I'd tried to fill in some gaps for her, but how could you possibly explain everything from the fall of the Soviet Union to the rise of social media?

I poured the water over the waiting coarse-ground coffee. I didn't tend to eat a big breakfast on market days, preferring to barter for a few delicious treats from fellow vendors instead. I pulled out a container of plain yogurt from the fridge, and a jar of homemade granola from the cupboard.

"Morning," a sleepy voice said.

I turned to see Cassie, clad in nothing but one of my oversized t-shirts, which came practically to her knees. Her blond hair was a tangled bird's nest. "Nice bed head."

"What?" Her hands flew to her hair, and she laughed. "Oh. Yeah. You have a brush?"

"In the top drawer in the bathroom. There should be a spare toothbrush in there too." I held up the large mason jar of granola. "This okay for breakfast?"

"Mmm. Perfect." Her words were husky with leftover sleepiness, and I couldn't help watch her walk away.

That was…easy.

Not exactly a reassuring thought. The ease with which I experienced her presence when everyone else in my whole life made me jumpy, how she made me joke the way I'd only ever been able to with my family…

It was like my soul remembered her.

Oh, no. Not going there.

I pushed the plunger down on the coffee press so swiftly that the press slipped off the counter, slamming on the floor, where it unceremoniously cracked, spilling wet grounds and freshly brewed dark roast all over the hardwood.

I grabbed a handful of tea towels from the drawer and starting mopping up my mess, throwing towels into the sink to rinse out later.

"What happened?" Cassie stood over me; I could feel her gaze.

"Nothing. I just dropped it, okay?" I slapped another soaked towel into the farmhouse sink.

"I'll help."

"Don't. There might be glass."

"I'll be careful."

She picked up the smashed press. "Huh. That's different." She held it over the sink where remnants of coffee dripped. "I don't think there are any loose pieces of glass, though. It's cracked, but none of the pieces are missing."

"Lucky me. Still ruined. Like everything else." I grabbed the trash can and she tipped the press into the sink to empty it of liquid, then gently tucked it into the plastic bin.

"Nicholas," she said. Her voice, heavy with an accent that hinted of origins even further South than my own, ensnared me, tendrils of raw silk wrapping around me.

"What?" The word came out clumsy, heavy.

She waited until my gaze locked with her eyes—green, like the most vibrant of moss, or the newest of spring grass. "I feel it too. The lostness. The vast emptiness. Yesterday, for me, it was another decade, another era. This house was full of coven sisters' laughter and Ginny's wisdom. I can't…"

Her pain swept over me like a wave. I wasn't an empath, but with Cassie, I felt everything. It wasn't just my own pain that ripped through me.

"You were running."

She studied me. "Running?"

"From someone who hurt you."

She nodded.

"Someone you feared."

"Yes." Unshed tears, heavy in that single word.

"Goddess, Cassie. I would. I would…" What could I say? Do anything to protect you? Stupid, freaking, cliché moron.

"I know."

"You feel it too?"

"I do." She shifted, moving closer to me.

I brushed my fingers through the tangles of her hair, impossible to smooth out, but beautiful in their disarray. "Sweet earth mother."

Her lips parted, and her hunger hit me, fused with my own, two storms merging into an unstoppable force.

The moan she gave as my lips met hers had me drawing her close. Her arms wrapped around my neck.

I pressed her against the kitchen island, my body rocking against hers. My tongue slipped into her mouth, and she arched, meeting the force of my kiss with her own.

She arched her body into mine, a sweet demand. My erection was throbbing. When she parted her legs, I slipped my leg between them. She wore nothing underneath my gray t-shirt, her bare pussy writhing wet against my skin.

"Nick!"

There was something startled in that word, not a cry of pleasure but one of panic. I stepped back, releasing her, my body shaking.

Her face was flushed, her breath rapid. She pressed a hand to her chest, then removed it and straightened the hem of the t-shirt. "I'm not…I'm sorry…I've given you the wrong impression."

She turned and fled down the hallway, followed by the sound of a door shutting firmly behind her.

I raked my hands through my hair, then finished cleaning up the coffee mess. In my bedroom—the furnishings spartan, to say the least—I threw on a pair of jeans and a blue t-shirt emblazoned with the farm logo I'd designed. Outside, I backed the pickup truck up to the barn doors and busied myself tossing bins of produce into the bed—a little more roughly than necessary.

Long after desire faded, magic buzzed under my skin, in my ears, in my head.

There was a newness to it, and an oldness, that I didn't much care for.

❋

Cassie

Behind the bathroom door, my knees gave way.

I squeezed my eyes shut, pressing my palms to the cool tile, grounding myself. Magic whipped around me, a frenzied storm building, traces of Nick's magic mixed with mine. If we ever…

Goddess. If we ever, it would be my undoing. My body shook.

Think about something else. Anything else.

I tried to unstick my tongue. I used to recite long lists of stitch and fabric types when my magic flared, but this? This wasn't just magic.

This was lust.

That was new territory. Not the awkward, clumsy offering in the backseat of a car at lovers' lane, but something unbridled. Natural. Sacred, even.

I remember Tricia, almost a decade my senior, whispering about it to me once. "The dance of the goddess and god. Raw, powerful, sticky, like honey dripped on your skin."

Sarah, another sister, a couple years older than me, had waggled her eyebrows. "And then licked off." They giggled, and I with them, though I'd never known any-thing like that.

But with Nick? Oh, yeah, I got it. Sweet, sticky honey. No.

I brushed my teeth so hard my gums ached, splashed water on my face, and rather viciously combed my hair.

I'd washed out my dress last night and thrown it over the shower rail. It had been little use—the pale fabric was stained and tattered beyond saving—but it was all I had. I tugged Nick's t-shirt off over my head, then shimmied back into the dress.

The kitchen was clean and empty when I entered.

A glance out the window revealed Nick across the yard near a green, battered pickup with farm use plates, loading crates into it with a great deal of…well, vigor.

Hadn't he said something about a market today? The kitchen was clean, and thoughts of breakfast had obvious-ly been abandoned. I dug around in the hall closet until I found a pair of black rainboots. They were clearly Nick's and far too large, but I stuffed paper towels inside until they were manageable.

I clomped outside. "Can I help?" I placed my hands on my hips, waiting.

Nick barely glanced at me. "In that?"

"It's all I've got."

"I can manage." He hefted a bin full of crookneck squash into the bed, turning his back to me to grab another.

I marched around the truck and grabbed a bin of new potatoes, their skin still speckled with earth, and carried it to the truck bed. "I said I was sorry." The words flew out of my mouth.

He stiffened. "Well, don't. You don't apologize for not wanting to have sex with someone, okay?"

I studied him, my chest and cheeks burning. "Good to know."

He stopped and wiped his hands on his jeans. "I'm not mad, Cassie. Not at you, anyway. You're...you haven't..."

The blush on my cheeks turned to fire. I felt it burning there. "Once. It wasn't...like that."

"He hurt you?"

"Not physically."

"Break your heart?" His words were gentle.

I met his gaze. I'd never trusted anyone with this story. "He used me. He tricked me into thinking he loved me because he heard I was a witch and wanted to see what it would be like."

"That bastard."

"Don't talk like that."

"Well, it's true."

Nick brushed his fingers against my jaw, settling a firm touch against my chin. "I would never hurt you. I'm a mess, Cassie, but I'm an honest mess, at least. I won't...I won't do that to you. You need to get back home. I'll help you find a way. You don't belong here."

"What if I do?"

"You don't."

I spun away, pressing a hand to my aching chest. "Okay."

Keep busy. Idle hands do the devil's work, like Mama said. I grabbed another bin of potatoes and carried it to the bed. I set it on the tailgate and jumped up to arrange it among the others.

Nick seemed to get that the conversation was over. Wordlessly, we settled a blue tarp over the produce and he grabbed some cords to secure it.

A shadow fell over me, though the sun still shone

above. There were no traces of clouds in the clear, blue, Virginia sky. Birdsong fell away.

Nooooo. A pained moan.

There was a crack, as of bones breaking. A horrible scream followed, and a wave of immense pain. I crashed to my knees.

"Cassie!"

Nick's voice was distant.

Power of thorn. From your body torn.

Power of stone. I'll sit on the throne.

A dark chuckle, the voice deep and masculine.

All mine, you bitch.

My eyes flew open. Nick was clutching me in the grass, stroking my sweaty skin.

"There's a reason." I swallowed, hard, fighting the bile that rose in my throat.

"For what?"

"For me. For us."

I closed my eyes against my pounding head. The shadows had fallen away, and the sun hurt.

He seemed to know, brushing my hair away from my face with the tenderest of touches. "What's that?" he whispered.

I pressed my hand to my head. "I don't know yet. But I will."

CHAPTER FIVE

Nick

"Are you sure you don't mind?" Cassie adjusted the belt around her waist and wiggled into the passenger seat.

I leaned back against the headrest. *Clear your head. Clear your mind.*

No. I'd never had a mind that was clear. Even before that night. Being around Cassie made magic sing in me, but I wasn't going there. Not after what happened.

"It's okay. You really shouldn't be alone. You just fainted."

"It was a trance."

"That caused you to faint."

"I don't need a babysitter."

Goddess, she was stubborn. No, I wasn't looking forward to showing up at the farmers' market with a mystery girl for everyone to gawk at. But man, I kind of wanted to see her face light up when she saw the market. I kind of wanted to walk down Main Street and show her all the new places.

I watched her fidget with the makeshift outfit I'd helped her throw together. "You look good." The words slipped out, innocent and yet...not at all intended.

A blush crept into her cheeks. "In my ruined dress?"

"Mom's kimono hides the worst of the stains."

Cassie glanced down, studying the blue floral print as if reading the tea leaves at the bottom of a cup. She fussed a bit with the lace trim at the bottom of the elbow-length sleeves. We'd scrounged up the kimono to cover her stained dress and even managed to find a pair of Gran's old flops. They were decidedly too much flop for Cassie's dainty feet, but maybe we could stop somewhere on the way home...

Home. This wasn't her home. This wasn't her time. And, like some lovesick fool, I'd made the ridiculous promise to help her find her way back to 1974. That wasn't how reality—not even our magical reality—worked.

"Okay." She clicked her seatbelt into place, smoothed her dress, and looked forward. "Okay."

I curled my fingers. I wanted to touch her. I wanted to show her what it was like to be with someone who cared, with someone who wanted to give pleasure.

But I was a mess. She needed someone a lot more together than some guy who came apart at the seams every time it rained.

The truck bounced down the gravel drive, and I made the familiar turn onto Chestnut Hollow Lane, headed toward town. I kept my eyes on the road, clenching and unclenching my hands on the wheel. Driving was one of the few activities that allowed me to relax a little.

I turned on the radio and switched it over to the CD player—the truck was too old to have a way to connect my phone, so I had to old-school it. The indie folk sounds of Backyard Misfits filled the cab. The lead singer's voice was scratchy and raw, the guitar gentle.

"This is good." Cassie rolled her window down, and out of the corner of my eye I saw her blond hair sweep up in a careless breeze.

"This is one of their best." We rode in silence as the music played.

"You have a good voice." There was a throaty quality to Cassie's voice.

I snapped my jaw shut. "Have I been singing long? Didn't even realize I was."

She shifted. "Just this last song. Is it your favorite?"

"Yeah." I clenched the steering wheel. "And under the stars I find her, and under the stars she's mine. And under the moon she finds me, and under the moon I'm hers."

"It's lovely."

"I think so." There was a tightness in my chest. I didn't even sing around my family.

"What's wrong?"

I shrugged. "Nothing."

"I like that you sing."

"Do you sing?"

She shook her head. "My parents weren't fond of singing. They believed in work. I learned to sew instead."

"Did you make your dress?" Subject change. Nice.

"Yeah. I make most of my own clothes."

"I don't know anybody who does that. Bet you and Gran got along."

"I'd help her with her quilts from time to time, do some of the detail stitching. One night, my first winter here, I got stuck at the farm for a couple days after the Long Nights Moon in December. There was a blizzard, and we sewed quilt squares the whole time, just drinking cocoa with cinnamon and talking. She was the first one who ever saw me, you know? I mean, she really saw me. All of me—my magic, my pain, my joy…all of it."

"That was her gift." The rest of the words clung to my throat, too painful to speak: *She was that for me too. She saw me.* "Which quilt did you make?"

Cassie leaned back, her long hair wind-tangled. "It was a green quilt with a pine tree over a backdrop of navy-blue mountains. For seeds not yet planted, Ginny said, and for dreams not yet dreamt."

"What?" My throat was drier than the Arizona desert that would soon enough be my home.

"What's wrong?" She frowned at me.

The words wouldn't come.

"Road, Nick—you're driving!"

"Crap." I swerved back into my lane. No one was coming, thank the goddess. "That was my quilt."

The color drained from her face.

I pulled into the parking lot of Harkness Pharmacy, my stomach aching. I squeezed my eyes shut. I'd lost my faith. Abandoned by the goddess and god. Haunted by the death of my coven. But even a lost witch like me knew that there were countless threads of destiny woven into our everyday lives.

And Cassie and I…it appeared our destinies were far more entangled than I could have ever imagined.

My breath came in shallow, painful waves.

Distantly, I heard her seatbelt unclick, and then she was drawing my head against her chest. Her fingers were in my hair, brushing the stubble of my short beard. Her lips brushed my temple.

"Why?" I said, my voice cracking.

"I don't know." She held me like an ailing child, and I let her. I didn't even care. It had been so long since I'd let anyone in.

Waves of air magic caressed me the way a summer breeze toys with the laundry on the line. A whiff of lavender carried from the kimono wrapped around her.

I drew away from her and met her eyes. "Is the world coming undone? Do you feel it too?"

Her lips parted. She shook her head. "I feel it. Something a long time coming. And we're a part of it."

I exhaled. The glaring numbers on the truck's clock reminded me I was cutting it close for getting to the market on time.

I could've turned around. A small part of me wanted to hightail it back to the farm, unravel the mystery.

But Cassie's magic called to my own sleeping magic.

And I wasn't ready.

I was out of words, so I put the truck in drive and headed the last few blocks to the market.

❋

Nick

The farmers' market wasn't yet packed, but I was getting a late start. Nancy and Russell Patters, who owned Mad Moon Roastery, shared a neighboring stall. They were already sipping their signature cold brew coffee behind a traveling display case filled with homemade bagels, muffins, and the best sourdough this side of the Mississippi.

I inclined my head toward them and started hauling out crates. Cassie didn't even ask, and she didn't hesitate to help. I unfolded a few tables.

Cassie cocked her hip against a blue bin of yellow squash. "Should I arrange these on the table?" She inclined her head to the one I'd just covered with a blue tablecloth.

"Yeah. That would be good." I didn't miss seeing Nancy nudge Russell in the ribs, nor the shrug he gave his wife while eyeing me and Cassie curiously.

It didn't even take half the time it usually took to prep my stall, maybe only a quarter.

Only because I was in a hurry, I reasoned. And because I couldn't stand the gawkers. That was why.

As the market filled with people, I felt as though damned near everyone was eyeing me and Cassie. I reached into my pocket and pulled out a twenty. "Cass," I said, leaning toward her.

She smiled up at me, brushing damp hair away from her face. "Yeah? We make a good team, don't we?"

Actually, we did. "Uh-huh. I could use a cup of coffee and maybe a pastry. French Twist Bakery has the best breakfast sandwiches in town. Do you want to go eat something, maybe bring me something back afterward?"

She eyed the Patters' stand with its chalkboard sign advertising coffee and baked goods but shrugged. "Okay." She took the twenty from my hand and wadded it up in her fist. "I guess I'll be back."

"I just don't want you to be bored, is all."

She met my eyes. Hurt. I'd hurt her. That didn't take long. "I wasn't. Where's French Twist?"

I gestured across the market with its square of stalls surrounding a courtyard filled with benches and potted geraniums. A willow tree stood in the center, stretching out her bowing branches with welcoming shade. "Just across the street. You'll like it. It used to be..." Her face paled as she stared in the direction I'd pointed.

"The Buttercup Diner," she finished.

"Yeah." I had memories of the former diner, but they were old ones, like me and Evan sharing a hot-fudge sundae on a Saturday afternoon, sitting on a cracked red vinyl bench.

Back when Dad was still around.

She shook her head. "Wow. Everything is so different." Her eyes took in the crowded market—babies in carriers peered out over their parents' shoulders; a rambunctious labradoodle tugged on its leashing, nearly pulling a teenage girl onto her backside.

Cassie didn't turn back to me, but merely strode across the market. I watched her until the door to the bakery shut behind her.

"Morning, Nick," Russell said. I turned to see him offering a compostable-plastic cup of cold brew with cream.

I took it and sipped, welcoming the splash of dark roast and ice against my tongue.

"Who's your lady friend?"

I shifted in place. "Just a friend. From college."

Nancy handed the teenager with the labradoodle a cold brew and a brown paper bag, then cast me a glance. "She seems nice. Reminds me of someone I used to work with years ago when I waitressed." She tucked a handful of ones into a metal lockbox. "Isn't it funny how that goes? You see someone who's the spitting image of someone from your past."

"Like that fellow we met in Richmond at that roasters' convention last year, Jeff something," Russell offered. "Wasn't he the spitting image of your cousin Charlie?"

Nancy nodded, her gray braid bobbing up and down against her floral peasant top. "Exactly. Isn't that something?"

Something inside of me unclenched, even though the fear was ridiculous. Who would suspect Cassie was a time-traveler? No, that wasn't our main concern. I wasn't so much worried that people would know she was from the past, but that we didn't know why she was here, in this time.

"You two serious?" Nancy asked.

"Nancy Jocelyn, don't ask the boy that. You're making him blush." Russell shook his head at his wife.

Yeah, my cheeks were hot. "We're friends. That's all." The flashes of that morning's encounter in the kitchen looping in my mind didn't help me sound all that convincing.

"Hmm," Nancy said, confirming my assessment of my half-assed lie. She turned to address a market-goer who wanted half a dozen bagels and something gluten-free for a houseguest, launching into a spiel about her gluten-free lemon bars with a great deal of gusto. That was the best part of farmers' markets. No one was in it for the money. We all did it because we loved what we did—growing, baking, cooking, canning, beekeeping, you name it. This was a place where passion came to find a home.

Russell leaned over the tables between us. "None of my business, son, but I saw the way you looked at her. I bet she'd be good for you, is all. Not right, you up at that farm all by yourself. Everybody needs someone."

Oh, goddess. Did everyone in this town have an opinion about my life? "If you break into song, I'm leaving."

Russell chuckled and threw up his hands. "Fair enough."

And then the market was in full swing—cars vying for precious parking spots, children laughing, friends and strangers alike chatting over cold brew and lemonade, old women haggling over the price of local honey.

"Hi, Jolly Old Saint Nick," a familiar voice said.

I swung around from the cash box to see Bailee Dugan. "You're back."

Clad in a halter dress that flared at the bottom, her black hair currently streaked with magenta, and a pair of cat-eye glasses perched on her nose, she pouted. "You could try to sound a little excited."

I shrugged. "Sorry. It's just…I didn't figure you'd ever come back."

"Well, Gram's house was just sitting empty, and I just finished my master's of library science, and they offered me Emmie Burdock's position."

I frowned. "What happened to Emmie?"

"She's retiring." Bailee leaned forward, waggling her eyebrows. "Word is, she found herself a gentleman lover down in Florida."

I snorted. Leave it to Bailee to be up on the town gossip. "When did you get back?"

"July 1."

"And you're just now saying hi?"

"You know how it is, Saint Nick. Leaky roof. Gutters falling off the house. Quite a state. Let's just say, I've learned not to climb a ladder in my bare feet, and thanks to an online tutorial, I can now install a new flapper on a toilet. Not nearly as interesting as a flapper from the speakeasy days, but hey, now the toilet works better." She stopped speaking suddenly. "And I'm rambling. What's new with you?"

"Same old."

Nancy leaned over the stall. "He's got a girlfriend."

Bailee's eyes widened. "Someone I know?"

"No one knows her. She's from…out of town." I fidgeted. Like me, Bailee had been affected by what happened that fateful night—she'd lost her grandmother too.

However, with Nancy clearly eavesdropping, I couldn't exactly talk openly with Bailee. That meant Cassie's time-traveling origins were off the table. I lowered my voice and mumbled hurriedly, "You'll have to come by and meet Cassie. I don't know how long she'll be in town for, though, before she goes…back."

Bailee nodded. "I will." She glanced over her shoulder. "I've got to run. My friend Vi and I are taking a yoga class in that new studio above the co-op." She adjusted her crossbody bag over her shoulder and leaned forward. "You feel it, right?"

I sighed. I could pretend that I didn't, but Bailee was a fellow witch. I gave a slight nod. "I do. Just don't know what it is."

She waved and hurried off to catch up with her friend.

A couple with three kids in tow stopped by, bought a few items, and asked for some farming tips. Even as I weighed produce, swiped cards, and counted out change, I couldn't keep my thoughts from straying to Cassie, to the way her long hair tangled around her face, to the way her lips had caressed my name in a half-sigh this morning.

And to the fact that she was a mystery I wouldn't mind spending the rest of my days unraveling.

CHAPTER SIX

Cassie

My breath caught as the door closed behind me. It wasn't that I'd just entered a place that should have been familiar, yet had been made foreign seemingly overnight. It was Nick, the slight country twang of his voice, the blond stubble that graced his cheek, the way I wanted to feel its roughness beneath my palm. And Goddess, he'd be my undoing.

He was getting under my skin all too quickly.

I sucked in a breath, clenching the twenty-dollar bill in my fist, and tried to adjust to the disorientation of entering what had only yesterday been Buttercup Diner—at least to me. The chrome stools with their red vinyl were gone, replaced with black wooden stools. The matching booths were gone too, and in their place sat granite-topped tables with sleek black chairs. The walls were cherry red and decorated with artwork that appeared to be for sale.

The scent of warm, buttery pastries and freshly brewed coffee tickled my nose. I shifted, a fish out of water. No.

This wasn't the first time I'd started my life over. It was strange, this new-old place, but not unpleasant.

"Take a seat, hon," a dark-haired woman in her mid-twenties said as she wielded a tray of steaming drinks, some of which were topped with foam, and one with a healthy dose of whipped cream and a sprinkle of cinnamon. "Be right with you."

Well, Nick wanted his space. That was fine. I could figure out my next steps while sipping coffee. I slid into a chair near the window, watched a sleek silver coupe whoosh by. The market across the street was bustling. A trio of musicians were setting up near a wide willow tree. And Nick was engaged in an intense conversation with the couple selling coffee and baked goods at the stall next to his.

"Morning," the waitress said. Back in my Buttercup Diner waitressing days, we all had to wear the same starched uniform, but this woman wore a form-fitting pair of floral print pants, a breezy olive-green skirt, and a pale-blue crop top under her black apron. She slid a menu in front of me.

"Today's drink special is a vanilla iced mocha. Pastry of the day is Alva's own pecan shortbread. Breakfast special is an egg white omelet with goat cheese and a side of rosemary potatoes."

My stomach growled at the list of specials, loud enough that my hand flew over top of it. If the waitress heard it—Paige, her nametag read—she didn't say anything. "The breakfast special sounds good. And two black coffees, one to go, one for here."

"We've got three brews today. The Mountain Mama is a dark roast. The Magpie is a medium roast, and the Spring's Serenade is more of a light roast."

"Umm…I'm used to two pots. Black handle is regular.

Orange handle is decaf."

She laughed, not a mocking laugh, but something sweet and sincere. "Cool. I like that. Keeping it simple. It took me three weeks to memorize the coffee and tea offerings here." She leaned forward, conspiratorial. "And every time I figure it out, Alva changes it."

I laughed. "My boss was like that with the sandwich menu. So, maybe surprise me?"

"You got it." She sauntered away, chatting with a couple of teenagers at a nearby table. They all had those "phones" that Nick had, their faces glued to one, occasionally erupting in laughter.

I studied Nick across the street. He was helping an elderly woman load a box of produce into the trunk of her vehicle. He even opened the driver's door for her, closing it firmly after she was securely in her seat.

"You and Nick, huh?"

I jumped a little as Paige slid a large, black coffee cup in front of me. "I…"

"No secrets in Willow Creek. Not for long." She cocked her head and watched Nick jog across the market back to his stall. "He's…been through a lot. You know about his family?"

I shrugged and busied myself pouring creamer into my coffee. "A little."

"My little sister went to high school with him. I think he took almost every single photo in their high school yearbook. Always had a camera in front of his face." She smiled. "Don't break his heart, okay?"

"I wasn't planning on it."

The table of teens erupted in raucous laughter, and she walked over, shushing them. Just like that, our conversation was over.

A few minutes later, I was devouring eggs and potatoes like I hadn't eaten in, well, forty-five years. The dish
had just the right amount of salt and herbs, enough to be
flavorful without overwhelming the taste of egg white and
starchy potato fried in butter.

"Anything else?" Paige asked. Her eyebrow nearly hit
the ceiling. "Wow. You were hungry."

"Yeah." I wiped my mouth with a napkin. "Nothing
else. Everything was fantastic. Just the check and that to-go
coffee. Oh, sorry, maybe a breakfast sandwich?"

She rattled off a list of options for the sandwich, and I
blindly answered.

A few minutes later, she slid a to-go cup, a brown
paper bag, and the check in front of me.

My eyes almost popped out when I saw the price—
this would be a fancy dinner in 1974—but I uncrumpled
the twenty as best I could and waited for Paige to return
with the change.

The diner disappeared. An image flashed in my head.
I was kneeling in the forest behind Ginny's farm, a black
candle burning.

I almost heard the words I'd spoken back then; the
spell almost came into form in my memory...

The vision vanished. I blinked a few times, the scene of
the diner coming into focus in front of me.

"I brought you an extra to-go cup of coffee. Thought
you might like to try the Magpie roast. Whoa." Paige slid
two paper cups in front of me. "You all right?"

"I'm fine. A bit sleepy, is all."

"Tell Nick, Lauren's sister says hi."

"I will."

I stood and tried to stretch as discreetly as possible, but
my body was heavy, as though from sleep.

Outside, the hot summer air slammed into me. The Virginia mountains weren't nearly as hot and humid as Georgia, but the heat could still pack a punch. I slid into a bench in the shade and watched a man in a red pickup truck parallel park as I sipped my coffee. *Think I liked the Magpie better than the Mountain Mama.*

Huh. Never thought I'd have to think a thought like that.

A prickling sensation tickled the back of my neck. I turned to find a woman watching me. Her red hair was tied back in a loose bun, her outfit casual, yet romantic— blush pink; a piece of amethyst on a long silver chain. And she simply stood there, staring at me.

I gave a half-wave. Maybe the rumors were spreading already.

Her hand flew to her oversized bag.

And then she turned away.

I sipped my coffee and turned away from her retreating form. Something seemed to tug on me, the way a crackling fire draws you closer on a frosty night. She and another woman disappeared around the corner.

I definitely wasn't in my element here.

The band started, banjo's twang, lively guitar, and a bit of drumming. The couple next to Nick's stall did a Texas two-step, out of sync with the music, but quite joyful. I tapped my foot in time to the music. A little boy danced under the willow tree, clearly a ham, basking in the attention his improvised dance moves got him.

From here, even Nick's shoulders seemed to relax a little, his smile less forced, easier, his brow less furrowed. I felt a little lighter too. Willow Creek was different, yet the same.

What happened to lead him to this place, where he'd walled himself off from everyone?

He's not alone in that. You ran away.

Ugh. My inner voice of hard truths. That was different, wasn't it? I was running from people who wanted me to hide my magic, from a brother who bullied me and parents who wanted to lock me away.

What happened to Nick to hurt him? What happened to cause the entire Willow Creek Coven, save Nick, to die?

And why did he fear the rain?

As if on cue, shadows fell over the sun. Big, fat plops of rain fell. A wild wind rushed past. I stood, but the wind was so strong I could barely walk forward. People gathered under the green roof of the market, but the musicians, stalwart, kept playing.

The flash of lightning was sharp, blinding. When it passed, after at least ten long seconds, everyone seemed frozen in place.

I blinked, adjusting to the shadows where once there had been sunlight.

A woman stood in front of the willow, her hair a tangle of roots and moss. Her dress, which looked understated and yet elegant, was torn and covered in dark stains.

Blood.

She met my eyes. "I brought you here for a reason, Cassandra. All of this will vanish. This is the magic of Willow Creek. Love, people, family. The four elements dancing in harmony, even for those who don't know magic exists. You and Nick will lead the charge."

"What charge?" A memory tugged at me like a forgotten dream, but I couldn't make the memory coalesce.

She raised her hands. They were ragged and bloody, as though the bones had been broken again and again. "He's taken me. He's taken me, and you have to save me."

"Who are you?"

"The Guardian."

"Wake up." It was a man's voice, threatening and furious—and didn't seem directed at me. The Guardian's head was tilted back as though forced. She faded from sight.

Everyone around me was still frozen in place—musician's fingers paused mid-chord on the strings; melting drips of ice cream paused halfway to the ground.

The ground trembled, and people began to talk. No one seemed to have noticed the strange moment.

I was a witch, but even for me, that moment had been disturbing.

The thunder that inevitably chases lightning shook the street. Another fork of lightning followed, aiming straight for the willow. It all happened so fast.

The tree crashed down, and an image flashed through my head: an oak tree in the storm, and the fall.

Oh, Goddess. Sweet Goddess.

I fell to my knees.

Helpless, I watched the musicians drop their instruments and run as the willow's limbs faltered and fell, as even the trunk toppled. A woman screamed.

Everyone ran, but Nick made it there first. Somehow, faster than I'd ever seen anyone move, he was diving under that tree.

The crashing of limbs settled. An eerie stillness fell. Soft, drizzly rain replaced the heavy downpour.

Oh, Goddess.

I ran across the street, not even bothering to check for cars.

"That was close," one of the musicians said.

"Carter!" A woman let go of a stroller and ran toward the tree.

"There's people under there!" a man shouted.

The man from the coffee stand and others nearby began clearing limbs. I pushed my way through.

Mother Goddess, protect them. In my mind, I let the chant echo, my magic whispering through my veins and pouring out into the world like a gentle, healing breeze—even though I felt far from gentle.

The crowd cleared the largest of the limbs with a heave.

Nick was hunched over the little boy. He raised his head and stood on shaky feet.

The little boy stood, his blue eyes wide. His mother pushed through the crowd and scooped him up. "Tree fell down," he said, and she hugged him with a mother's ferocity.

I ran to Nick, stood before him, not caring that half the town was watching. "Are you okay?"

He brushed himself off. "Yeah. I'm fine." He glanced at the woman. "Is Carter okay?"

She nodded.

I cupped Nick's chin, examining every inch of his face. "You're going to have a bruise."

He shrugged. The crowd's shock had turned to a roar of frantic conversation, but my eyes were on Nick. "You are fierce, Nicholas Felson. Fierce, and beautiful beyond words."

I kissed him, slow and deep.

People were watching.

People *would* be talking.

Hades and hellhounds, but I didn't even care.

CHAPTER SEVEN

Nick

My head spun, and I almost wished I could do that thing the wizards in *Harry Potter* did, though I couldn't remember what they called it. If I could, I would've whisked Cassie right out of there, in the blink of an eye, to somewhere we could continue that kiss.

The sirens were what drew us apart. Two sheriff's deputy vehicles, the fire department's brand-new fire truck, and Willow Creek's only ambulance pulled up to the market.

Deputy Chris Harding, a classmate of mine from my Willow Creek High days, stepped out of his vehicle and slammed the door. "Clear the area!" His shout did little to disband the maddening crowd.

I grabbed Cassie's hand, our fingers easily entwining, and we stepped away from the jagged remains of the willow tree. While Chris rummaged around in his trunk and glared at the crowd, the other deputy, Kirsten Powell, straightened her brimmed deputy's hat over her neat blond hair and began guiding confused market-goers away from the scene.

Chris shut the trunk and emerged with a bullhorn. Kirsten caught my eye, and we just shook our heads. Chris meant well; he just didn't do subtle. She jogged over to him, he nodded sharply, and then he opened the trunk again, this time grabbing the caution tape.

The weight of Cassie's gaze drew mine to hers. "Did you see her?" she asked.

"See who?"

"The Guardian."

"The Guardian? Of Willow Creek? No. No one sees her, Cassie. We feel her, but..." Oh. Wow. I kept my voice deliberately low. "You saw the Guardian? Just now?"

She nodded, her expression pained. I wanted to kiss her pain away, but that would have to wait. "You felt the magic, though?"

"It was...there was a darkness. It hurt, like hearing the world's most poorly tuned, out of sync orchestra. I felt it scrape against me." My stomach twisted. I thought I might be sick. The charred willow, the town's centerpiece, lay in twisted ruins. Even now, a sickly stench of charred magic wafted up, vaguely sulfuric.

But tangled there, too, amid the wisps of sharp shadows, was the light, airy feel of Cassie's magic, wrapping around me. And my earth magic, green as moss with streaks of amber, that prehistoric sap crystallized after millennia into one of nature's countless masterpieces... Oh, yes, my magic danced with hers, sweet and heavy and aching after so long without use. Cassie's presence was like the promise of birdsong that would meet my ear on a warm summer morning if only I opened the window.

But there was a foul darkness here. It had almost taken a little boy's life. The EMTs were checking him out now, though we'd been fortunate.

One of the EMTs, a younger man I didn't recognize, came toward me. "I'd like to take a look at you, if that's okay."

I shook my head. "I'm fine. Really."

"Got an abrasion on your cheek."

"It'll heal."

"At least let me examine you briefly."

"I'm fine." I grit my teeth. "Really."

Kirsten was guiding people to their cars, and while Chris cordoned off the farmers' market with yellow caution tape, another newly arrived deputy was directing traffic.

Cassie stepped in. She smiled at the EMT. "I'll take care of him. Don't worry."

The guy looked torn. Finally, he shrugged. "Suit yourself. If he experiences any nausea, vomiting, confusion, call 911."

"I will."

There was a sharp whistle. "Out of there, Felson!"

I shot Chris a look, but wrapped my arm around Cassie's waist and guided her out of the market and toward my truck. We had to duck under a stretch of police tape. There would be no collecting the remains of my produce or dismantling my stand today. I opened the passenger door for Cassie and helped her in.

She smiled down at me. "You don't have to do that."

"Trying to be a gentleman."

She laughed. "Are you now?"

I shut the door and turned to see Chris standing there. At six-four and two-twenty, the guy loomed over me, just like he always had. He'd never bullied me, just always let me know with a laugh or an eyeroll that he thought I was a freak.

"Heard you saved that kid." The softness in his voice took me aback.

"I did what I had to do."

One corner of his mouth jerked up. "You remember Lauren Feldspar?"

"Yeah. Head cheerleader?"

"That's her. Anyway, she's teaching at the Montessori school in town and we're engaged. Fact is, we're more than engaged. We're having a baby."

"Congrats." I meant it, though I wasn't sure why he was spilling his guts to me, of all people—or why now, of all times.

"Just, on my way over here, I was thinking, I hope that kid's okay. And then they said it was you who saved him. I always thought…" He shook his head. "That maybe you thought you were better than us, being Ginny's grandson and all."

"Really?"

He grunted and looked away. "Well, maybe you're not so bad. I'll let you get going. Kirsten's going to have someone call the vendors when it's safe to come back and pick up everything. See you around."

I climbed in the truck and started it, grateful for the air conditioner's blast.

Cassie clicked her seatbelt into place. "What was that about?"

I shifted the truck into drive and headed back toward the farm. "I can honestly say I have no idea."

In less than twenty-four hours, a woman from nearly fifty years in the past had shown up at my doorstep, a magical storm had nearly torn apart the most popular Saturday morning gathering spot in town, and the guy who'd hated me since high school just told me his life story.

I reached for Cassie's hand. Already, I'd begun to rely on her.

But everyone I'd relied on in my life was gone now.

And Cassie didn't belong in my world.

So, where did that leave me?

Cassie

Nick was quiet on the drive back to the farmhouse, his lips twisted into the frown he'd worn last night, when he sensed my magic.

The farm seemed sleepy in the summer sunlight; the shutting of the car doors almost sharp in the quiet.

Too quiet.

Something wasn't right, and not just my time jump. My head was reeling because that short jaunt into town had shown me just how much everything had changed. The magic in Willow Creek was off. I should've felt it before. Slumbering. And yet…when Nick and I were together long enough, our magic collided like two stormfronts.

Nick unlocked the back door and we stepped inside. The screen door whooshed with a creaking and hissing of hinges, then with a clang as it finally shut. The air inside was blessedly cool, but I felt confined, cooped up.

I brushed my hair, now hopelessly tangled from the freak storm, away from my face.

Nick watched me.

I laughed. "What?"

"Crap. I don't even know."

"Say it." Despite the push and pull of Nick—drawn together one second, the next pushed away—I felt comfortable around him.

He turned, studying the oak table with its farmhouse chairs. A stained-glass chandelier hung above and a wide window looked out over the fields and the deep blue mountains beyond.

I approached him from behind and wrapped my arms around his waist. I'd never been this way before—so bold. Bold with magic? Yes. Bold with a man? Never.

But somehow, Nick made it okay. Even if he said no to something I did, I knew he'd be kind about it.

"These mountains, Nick. They're in you. In your voice, your heart, your soul. And in your magic."

I felt his breath quicken, though I couldn't see his face.

"That's what scares me."

"Why?"

"You don't know…" His voice cracked. "You weren't there that night. You didn't see what I saw."

"Do you want to tell me?"

I leaned my head against his back, my cheek against the damp fabric of his t-shirt. He sighed, and it rippled through me.

"You're exhausted," I said, and I didn't mean from the events of the day. "You've carried so much for so long."

His shoulder muscles jerked, then relaxed. "Yeah. Magic is an open secret in this town, you know. I've always felt like a freak."

I squeezed his waist and wiggled against him. "They love you."

"Who?"

"Everyone."

"That's just because I helped Carter."

"The little boy? No. Even before, the waitress—Paige, I think—she saw me looking at you. They don't love you because you're Ginny's grandson or Maeve's son. You're just a part of this town."

"She told you that?"

I smiled. "Not in those exact words, but something to that effect. And I saw that couple beside you, the way they talked to you."

He relaxed into silence. The afternoon sky was bright and cloudless, but there was a stillness in that which I found unsettling. I couldn't shake it. Something was waiting for us.

Nick shook off my embrace and turned. He gazed down at me—easily five-ten where I was scarcely five-foot. His expression was somehow fierce and gentle at the same time.

It set me on fire.

"Cassandra."

"Shit, Nick. Don't say my name like that."

He grinned. "You cursed. I didn't think you cursed."

A choked half-laugh escaped, breathy. "Around you, I'm different. Freer, somehow." My body shook, a faint tremor I couldn't begin to explain. "There's this magic. It's something old and something new at the same time."

He brushed his thumb against my jawline. "Something wonderful and something terrifying."

My lips formed an O. I pressed a hand to his chest, felt his heart pounding a wild rhythm. My legs shook. "We should…"

He slid his hands into my hair, massaging my scalp with his fingers in slow, entrancing circles. "We should what?" He leaned in and whispered against my ear. "Cassandra."

I leaned against the table for support. With Nick, there was a lot I didn't know, but I knew the kind of person he was. I knew he was honest and had a good heart. I knew he'd been through bad things and yet still kept hold of his goodness. And I knew that took courage.

I leaned up and kissed him. When we were both breathless, I drew away. "Make love. I want to make love."

He kissed my cheek. "Are you sure?"

"I'm so unbelievably sure."

He took my hand and guided me down the hallway. Last door on the right—Maeve's old room. We stepped inside. It was worlds different now. Three walls were stark white, the third, a deep navy blue, the décor sparse—black and white photos in worn wood frames on the walls, clothes scattered everywhere on the floor— yet there was somehow a fullness to it.

Nick wrapped his arms around my waist and slid the kimono down a little, kissing the spot where my shoulder and neck met. My thoughts vanished.

I moaned, my hand reaching back to slide along his thigh as he worked his way up and down one side of my neck, then the other. Heat pooled between my legs.

I stepped out of his grasp.

He frowned. "What's wrong?"

I smiled and unbelted the kimono. "I'm wearing too many clothes." The kimono slid in a featherlight whoosh to the floor. I toyed with the straps of my dress, sliding them down my shoulders slowly before I wiggled out of it. "Come to think of it, you're wearing too many clothes too."

I tugged his t-shirt over his shoulders, planted kisses on his chest. I could've spent a lifetime memorizing the contours of his muscles.

But then his hand slid up my thighs and then I was moaning, leaning against his solid weight as he fingered me. His hardness pressed against me and I unzipped his jeans, taking the bare length of him in my grasp.

His groan was deep, almost pained with pleasure. I smiled, liking that I was the cause of it.

He plunged a finger inside of me, and my eyes rolled back in my head.

"Please." I writhed against him.

"Now?"

I could only nod.

He drew away from me long enough to tug his jeans off, then reached into the nightstand and withdrew a foil package. I sat on the edge of the bed, my breath ragged. When he returned to me, his eyes were gentle. He leaned over my body and kissed me. I lay back on the bed.

"Are you sure?" he asked.

I smiled and leaned back into the softness of a pillow. "Oh, yes."

He kissed me, leaning on one elbow as he guided himself into me with his other hand. Nothing in my life could've prepared me for that feeling. I wrapped my legs around him, my fingers digging into his biceps. I heard my moans and his as though from a distance.

Pleasure built inside me, like a wave building until it crashed onto the shore. I screamed, the sound wild and freeing. Nick pressed his head against mine and shuddered his release.

In the quiet that followed, we lay there, our breath heavy, our sweaty bodies pressed together. He drew away just a little and kissed me. After a minute, he lay down beside me again and wrapped his arms around me, pulling my body against his.

My eyes grew heavy, my body sinking into the mattress. "Mmm."

He kissed my shoulder, then traced his fingers along my back.

We lay there in the quiet of a country summer afternoon, his fingers tracing abstract designs on my bare skin as I tried to catch my breath. Nothing in my life had prepared me for that.

Like honey dripped on the skin, then licked off.

Yes.

The patterns he traced on my skin began to form a shape. I wiggled, still under the spell of our lovemaking.

"Is that a tree?" I asked as he drew.

He nodded. "Not just any tree. It's the Lady in the Oak."

An image flashed in my mind. I sat up.

He sat up too, frowning. "What did I say?"

"The Lady in the Oak?"

"Yeah." He studied me. "It's just a story my grandmother made up for me and Evan, about a witch who was trapped in an oak tree in the woods. There was even an actual tree. The markings in the bark looked like a woman's face. Someday, in a time of great need, Gran said the Lady would be set free."

My stomach twisted. "Oh Goddess." I pressed my hand to the knot that had formed in my abdomen.

He took my hand. "What is it?"

I met his eyes. "I know how I got here. I think…I think I remember."

For a moment, we just sat there in the summer silence, our magic asleep and sated following the release of sex.

But we both knew. I saw it in his eyes, in the way he arched his neck, studying me like I was the Mona Lisa.

"You, Cassie? You're the Lady in the Oak?"

I nodded. "I think so."

CHAPTER EIGHT

Nick

Goddess. It wasn't possible. Cassie stood, her back turned to me, a twisted sheet wrapped around her body.

I swung my legs over the edge of the bed and rose, wrapping my arms around her and tucking her head under my chin. "Do you remember? What happened to you? How you got here?"

She shook her head but made no move to dislodge it from under mine. Instead, she leaned back. I kept my embrace firm, but not so tight that she couldn't pull away if she needed to.

Cassie stared ahead at the wall covered with black-and-white eight-by-ten portraits of my family—of Gran, her gray hair in a braid; of Mom, her long skirt billowing around her as she danced outside at one of our midsummer circles; and of Evan—not the cocky, sauntering figure he showed to the world, but another side. He was leaning over his guitar, his brow furrowed, his eyes hooded as he strummed, forgetting for the moment to play a part.

I hadn't realized it until this moment, but the only other photo on that wall was of the Lady in the Oak herself, leaves resplendent green on a summer day. I almost felt the scratch of bark under my fingers as I traced the shape that nature had made there—or so I'd thought.

I jutted my chin forward. "Look at the photo on the wall. That's her. The Lady in the Oak."

Cassie stepped forward, out of my embrace. She brushed her fingers against the frame I'd fashioned out of reclaimed barn wood. One hand clenched the navy-blue sheet around her body.

Like that first night—could it have only been less than twenty-four hours ago?—her pain hit me like a blast of wind.

There was no glass on the frame, and her slender fingertips trailed along the outline of the face—wild waves of hair, a slightly upturned nose, closed eyes, soft lips.

"Sweet Goddess, let me remember," she whispered.

A subtle magic shifted in the air—a whisper of wind, a vague and passing scent of lavender. Part of me wanted to run, to bolt and get the far away from magic as possible.

But I remained rooted was I was. That was what Cassie needed.

She whispered again, her voice deepening, the magic stirring again.

"Stop," I said, the word coming out a croak.

She turned to me, her eyes shimmering with unshed tears. "We have to know."

"I know." I stepped between her and the photograph and plucked it off the wall, tugged the quilt off the bed and laid it on the floor. "Wait right there, Cassie. I'll be right back."

Not caring about clothes, I went to the hall closet.

Truth was, I rarely opened it anymore except to get snow or rain gear, but that's where Gran kept the essential, bare-bones magic supplies. I returned with the patchwork bag she'd handsewn—gold fabric intermixed with navy blue, covered in gold stars and silver moons. The lining was sturdy black canvas, quilted to keep the contents a little more secure.

Cassie was nestled in the center of the quilt, the sheet wrapped to form a makeshift toga.

"I think we need to get you some clothes," I said, trying to lighten the mood—then almost laughing at myself when I realized that times were indeed tough if it was up to me to boost spirits.

But Cassie made it easy. She grinned, eyeing me from head to toe. "I don't know. I could get used to this."

"Agreed."

She quirked an eyebrow. "I see that."

I cleared my throat and thrust the bag toward her.

What the hell could I say? *Cassie, I could spend the rest of my life like this.* Me, Nick Felson, who'd never had a serious girlfriend? Someone who couldn't make a relationship last more than three months? *See a therapist.* That's what the last girl I dated said to me. But Cassie just *got* it. Really, truly understood.

Cassie took the bag and set it down. She seized my hand and tugged me onto the quilt. I settled in. Magic. Focus. Moving forward.

You always dwell on the past, Evan said. *Dad leaving. All that crap. The future is where it's at.*

"Before…" Cassie's voice was low, uncertain.

I clenched my jaw. "You mean, in bed?"

Her eyes widened. "No. Can I finish a sentence, please?"

"Okay."

"Before we do this. I don't know what lies on the other side of this magic, Nick. I just want to say thank you. That was, well, the word 'exquisite' comes to mind."

The tension in my jaw slackened. I took her hand and kissed it. "For me, too. You're special, Cassie. One of a kind."

"Well, I am a time-traveling girl from the seventies. I'd say that's pretty unique."

"Not just because of that. You're just the first person to ever really…" I shrugged.

"You're the same for me."

Gods. I didn't even have to finish a sentence with this girl. She would be my undoing.

Our eyes locked for a few seconds. She exhaled and shook her head, tangled blond hair framing her face. "Ready?"

No. No, I wasn't. What if what we unlocked sent Cassie tumbling back to her own time?

I squeezed her hand, and she studied me with those soft green eyes that belied her fierceness, her intensity.

"Okay. Whatever happens…" My throat was dry around the words I longed to say. What kind of fool said this kind of thing to a girl he'd just met? A man in the clutches of magic?

"I'm glad I met you," I finished, wincing at the sheer lameness of the words.

She kissed my cheek. "And I'm more than glad I met you. But maybe this isn't the end of our journey—just the next step."

She unzipped the bag and rummaged through the contents, selecting things, worrying her lower lip, muttering to herself, then putting things in and taking something else out. She settled on a bottle of rosemary essential oil, a black candle, and four small selenite wands.

With the oil, she traced a pentacle—a five-pointed star representing the four elements and the fifth, spirit—onto the candle. She placed a piece of selenite, a white, striated stone, at each of the four quarters—East, South, West, and North.

She dug through the bag and peered inside. "No matches."

"I got it." I pulled a lighter out of my drawer—silver, engraved with a rose.

"You smoke?"

"No. It was Mom's, back in the day. She gave it to me because she didn't think my brother could be trusted with it."

"Your brother. Was he a troublemaker?"

"Yeah. But he could talk his way out of anything."

"My brother was like that...with Mama and Dad, anyway."

"The same brother you said was looking for you back then?" I sat down, tracing my fingers over the engraved rose the way I'd done a thousand times before.

She nodded, twisting in her seat, brushing her hair behind her shoulders. "He was a very angry person. Maybe still is." She shrugged, faux-casual, but there was bitterness there. And fear.

"He hurt you?"

She shrugged. "No. He was just a bully. He was part of the reason I ran away after high school graduation. Packed a brown plaid suitcase and hopped on the next bus out of town."

"To Willow Creek?"

She shook her head. "To New York. But the bus driver got lost—really, really lost—and then the bus broke down outside the Buttercup Diner, just as Ginny and some of the sisters were leaving. She saw me and offered me a place to stay. I accepted." Cassie tilted her head back. "That was the first time I ever belonged anywhere."

"And now it's all gone."

"No." She shook her head and leaned forward, her face fierce. "No. It's so far from gone. You taught me that." She held out her hand. I set the lighter in her palm, and she flicked it open, the flame blossoming.

There was that all-too-familiar hiss as it hit the wick of the pillar candle. A twin flame bloomed there, and for a moment, twin salamanders—fire elementals—danced atop the flames. Cassie withdrew the lighter and snapped it shut with a flick of her wrist.

She settled into her seat, in simple cross-legged pose. I sat with my knees bent, lower legs tucked underneath. We inhaled and exhaled in unison, settling into the rhythm of meditation magic as though we'd done it our whole lives.

I love her.

The thought echoed in my mind, though it had nothing to do with the purpose of our meditation.

I blinked, but the bedroom had vanished. I was on a mountaintop—McCafferty's Point, actually, a peak overlooking the town of Willow Creek and one of the most difficult hikes in the region.

"I told you a long time ago that we don't get to choose what the goddess shows us, Nicholas."

I spun around.

There she was.

"Gran." I tried to run toward her, but I was rooted in place.

She shook her head. "Not yet. There will be a reunion, but now is not that time. This is not that place."

The moon was full, and summer air carried the scent of newly fallen rain, damp rock, pine forest. The town slept below.

Suddenly remembering my current state, I glanced down, grateful to see I'd donned a pair of black linen pants.

Gran chuckled. She had on a white tunic trimmed in gold, her pants billowy white linen. "Worried you might be journeying into the astral plane skyclad?"

I shrugged. "Something like that."

Her long gray hair was almost always braided, but tonight it was unrestrained, flowing in silvery waves down her back. The breeze caught it and sent it trailing behind her. She looked mystical, ancient, the way she did in ritual.

"I don't know, child, if my journey will bring me back to your world. At least not for long. I've suspected for a while now that there might be some new adventure on the horizon. But the others…They're waiting. Stuck and scared."

I stumbled backwards, but the magic of the vision caught me, steadied me. "I didn't know. If I had…"

Her gaze was soft. "You weren't meant to, love. Not until the time was right. I didn't know why the Guardian took Cassie all those years ago. Only that I was meant to wait. It was painful, feeling I'd failed her, but knowing that I had to let things play out. And then, leaving you, and feeling your pain from this great distance…I'd tried to prepare you. My only comfort was in knowing that Cassie would come to you soon enough, and you would know a great love."

"How could you possibly know that?"

There was a great rustle of wings from a nearby tree, and a barred owl flew past us and into the night.

Gran watched it with a soft, sad smile. "Something happened to me that night Cassie became one with the oak. I began to see how Willow Creek's destiny would unfold. It is a place where magic and the everyday have always been entangled. It's your job to bring the others back, to fight the darkness and see that doesn't change. You and Cassie will lead the coven soon."

"I'm twenty-three. Gods, Gran, Cassie is barely twenty."

"People far younger and less wise than the two of you have been called to much greater destinies."

Though I'd left my physical body back on another plane, my heart was in my throat. "Not me."

"Yes, you. And Cassie. The magic you two awaken will be fierce."

I smiled, sheepish. "It already is."

She laughed. "I figured. Not sure you've ever practiced magic skyclad before."

"Getting a little awkward, Gran."

She waved it off and turned away, standing at the cliff's edge and staring at the impossibly large disc of the moon. "The Black Moon is coming."

I struggled to remember the phrase, but it wasn't familiar. Every full moon had a name—the Long Nights Moon in December, the Strawberry Moon in June. But the Black Moon? I'd never heard of it.

Gran continued. "That will be the night when all is decided. Shrouded in darkness. Tonight, go with Cassie. Enter the Crossroads at the place you last saw me. Bring him home."

"Bring who? What's the…?"

But it was no use. She was gone.

Inky shadows of clouds swept across the moon until the mountaintop and the valley below were bathed in darkness.

Thunder rumbled.

I opened my eyes.

The candle flame glowed, unwavering in the bedroom.

Cassie opened her eyes and I stared at her, too bewildered to speak.

"I remember," she whispered. The fear in her voice shook me out of my post-trance stupor.

I swept her into my arms. "Tell me."

CHAPTER NINE

Cassie

I couldn't tell which of us was trembling harder. I drew out of Nick's arms, still shaky.

"I always crave chocolate after trance, don't you?" I said.

He smirked. "The darker, the better."

I stood, stretching, my body stiff. I didn't dare close my eyes. I didn't dare glance down at that heartbreakingly beautiful photograph, the one that connected two disparate threads of my life—a past that was forty-five years ago and also yesterday, and whatever lay in front of me and Nick.

I only knew now that I belonged here, with him by my side.

He tugged on his jeans. "Do you want to borrow something and we can throw your dress in the wash?"

I picked it up. "I think it belongs in the trash bin, to be honest."

He opened a dresser drawer and handed me a t-shirt emblazoned with the logo of a coffee company. From another drawer he withdrew a pair of sweatpants. "You could try folding over the waistband a few times and they might sort of fit."

I wrinkled my nose. "I think I'm going to need some new clothes eventually."

He nodded, his face darkening. Crap. Those simple words implied so many complicated things.

"I didn't mean…"

He crossed the room and kissed me, a brief, hard kiss. "I'll get us something to eat." With that, he buttoned his jeans and put on a t-shirt, then walked out of the room.

I fussed with the clothes. They were impossibly baggy, but they smelled like Nick—like patchouli, a hint of sandalwood, and the fresh scent of mountain air—so that was something.

I padded into the kitchen where Nick was pouring two glasses of iced tea and rummaging through the cupboards. A glance at the clock told me it was almost five. It felt like one of those days were time flew by, impossibly fast, and yet a million things had happened.

We sat at the kitchen table. I folded my feet into a simple cross-legged position. Nick stretched his out to rest on the chair across from him.

I polished off half of my mint iced tea in a few gulps. The ice rattled in the glass as I set it down.

He studied me, his gaze soft. "Do you want to tell me?"

I nodded, closing my eyes.

"It started when he found me. My brother. He was coming to Willow Creek to drag me home. And I couldn't let that happen. Home was…it was like a prison. No magic. I couldn't even go into the woods because Mama said there was too much temptation for magic there. And my brother Nathan? He was their enforcer. That night, I went to the forest to cast a protection spell, something to block him from finding me. I pushed really hard." My voice cracked. Nick's hand sought mine. I turned his palm in my hand, my thumb worrying the callouses it found there.

"He showed up—Ginny hot on his heels. He was going to take me back home whether I wanted to go or not. I begged the Guardian to protect me. And she did—for a price."

"That's how you came to be asleep in the oak tree for all those years?"

Nick held out a bar of chocolate, broken into tiny squares, and I took one. I bit into it, swallowed, then took another delicious bite, letting the rich taste refresh my body.

"Yes. She saved me, but in doing so, she brought me into the future." I eagerly took another piece of chocolate, my body grounding into this time, this reality, as I ate. "She said she had a reason. I just don't know what it is. Not yet."

Nick washed down a square of chocolate with the last of his iced tea. "I do."

He rose and grabbed the pitcher of tea from the fridge, topping off each of our glasses. He took a few sips, then traced the condensation on the outside of the glass with his fingers. "Gods, Cassie. You've been through so much. And you're still...how do you have this lightness about you when you've been through so much pain?"

"Because I'm stubbornly hopeful. It's the only thing that saved me. And now I know why."

He glanced away. A foreboding shadow slid over us, the kind only a witch could notice. It felt like a cold wind that hinted at snow.

I stood up, my chair scraping against the floor, and went to him. With my palm, I urged his face to turn toward me. "Your turn. Tell me what you saw."

"I saw her." There were tears in his voice. "My Gran."

My legs wobbled. My hands fell to Nick's shoulders, steadying myself. "Her spirit?"

"They're not dead. None of them." His voice cracked. "Goddess, Cassie. Something has them. It's up to us. We have to be the ones to bring them back."

I stumbled backward into my seat. "There's a chance that we can see them again?"

He nodded. A solitary tear slid down his cheek. He blinked and pressed his palms to his eyes.

After he'd had a moment to take a few deep breaths, I clasped one of his hands over the table. "I need to know how this happened. What happened to them?"

"I haven't told anyone before."

"You said they died."

"There was a wave of water, and then they were gone. We never found bodies, though." A tremor raked him. "Goddess."

He ran out of the room and down the hall.

I gave him a few minutes before I knocked on the bathroom door. He was sitting with his back against the bathtub, head in his hands.

"If you're not ready…"

"I don't have a choice."

I wanted to tell him that wasn't true, we always have a choice, but I remembered far too well all those years I didn't have one.

And I loved him too much to lie.

I sat down beside him, smoothing his mussed hair. His forehead was covered in a sheen of sweat, and I ran cold water over a washcloth and pressed it to his temples and cheeks.

"Thanks."

"That's what we do for the ones we love." My hand paused, clutching the washcloth as I held it against his right cheek. "I shouldn't have said that."

His gaze was intense, but somehow soft. "Why not? We both feel it."

"We do?" My body sunk into the softness of the bath rug.

He nodded. "I feel like I've known you my entire life. Like…"

"Like it's meant to be?" I wrinkled my nose. "How cheesy are we?"

"Oh, we're unforgivably corny."

I laughed. His laughter joined mine.

"Whatever it is, we'll face it together." I pressed the washcloth to his forehead, smoothing his hair back, my fingers massaging his scalp. I felt him relax under my touch, and we both fell into a soft sort of trance.

The daylight fell away, then, twilight's shadows slid over us. The air smelled of freshly baked bread and homemade roast—Ginny's famous recipe.

Somehow, I knew, we were sliding back through time again, into the magic of memory.

Not mine, this time. It was Nick's memory. His journey.

I was just in the passenger seat.

Nick
July 30, 2018

Gran stood at the farmhouse sink, finishing off the dinner dishes. We'd stayed late, chatting, as usual, and the July sun was already sliding behind the mountains. I accepted the casserole dish she handed me. There was no delineation of men's work and women's work in our family—we all did as was needed to see the day through.

Mom had already rushed off to the birthing center—twins, arriving two weeks early, and the mother-to-be wanted Maeve Felson there when her babies came. Everyone did. It wasn't just that folks trusted our family's magic. Mom was a skilled nurse-midwife. She worked hard and kept studying and taking classes long after she'd earned her credentials. And people liked her. She set everyone—mothers, fathers, even the babies themselves—at ease.

I toweled off the casserole dish.

Gran often hummed a favorite song as she worked—"Wild Mountain Thyme" was her particular favorite—but tonight her mood was as somber as a winter sky heavy with storm.

"Something's coming."

I studied the reddish twilight sky outside the window. "I don't think so. Red skies at night, sailor's delight."

"Not tonight." She closed her eyes, and it hit me—the weight of what she carried. Our coven—every witch's sorrows, joys, obstacles, triumphs. Folks came to her with their troubles, and she carried them. She'd guided generations of witches—Mom's, now mine and Evan's—along their magical paths.

She sighed. "I failed once, Nicholas."

I set the casserole dish on the bamboo drying rack. Only the pots and pans remained, and those could soak. "You mean, magically?"

She nodded and licked her lips. Tonight, for the first time, her wrinkles were heavy with sadness where I usually saw laugh lines. The crow's feet that spoke of wisdom seemed to speak of some long-kept burden. "Her name was Cassandra. She was lovely. You would've loved her."

I mentally shook my head at her strange choice of words, but I didn't dare interrupt. Gran knew my burdens well. Tonight, she needed to speak. I would listen.

She nodded. "I sensed she was troubled like…like someone else is now. I felt the magic shifting around her, saw the shadows lurking in her aura. Not her own darkness, but indeed a darkness had attached itself to her."

Gran met my eyes. Scared. I stepped back, slamming into the counter behind me. "The shadows are here. They've been there all along—I see that now. Whatever happens in the coming days, sweet Nicholas, remember: There's nothing left but to see it through. We must all be strong, whatever happens."

I tried to speak, to reassure her, but my throat was parched beyond speech.

The screen door swung open. Evan stepped in. His outfit was quintessentially Evan—black skinny jeans, a white t-shirt, a vintage black leather vest of Granddad's over top. He grinned.

"I saw it again, Gran."

She raised an eyebrow, back to her old self again. "Saw what?"

"You'll see." He adjusted the hairband holding his blond hair in its ponytail. He grinned that lopsided grin. "Want me to get my guitar out, Gran? You look tired."

"No. Nick and I just finished up the dishes—" She sent him a dirty look reminding him that he'd enjoyed the meal and skipped out on the cleanup, a violation of the family rules even ever-charming Evan would pay for later. "And we're going to sit on the back porch a while, aren't we, dear?"

"Yeah." I could take the hint. She wasn't game for Evan's machinations tonight. I grabbed a couple of glasses, added the ice, sweet tea, and lemon slices.

When I turned, two glasses in hand, Evan had seized Gran's hand. We were twins, but not identical. He was prettier, to be honest. Mom and Dad had met at the Thirsty Fiddler where Dad's band played every third Saturday, and Mom washed dishes to pay her way through nursing school—a wheeler-dealer type, Gran always said of him.

There was something strange in Evan's eyes tonight, a wildness that wasn't *his* wildness exactly. Evan was reckless and a playboy to boot, but tonight he seemed almost dangerous.

And Gran? Gone was the keenness in her gaze. She smiled softly at Evan, a doe-eyed look I didn't recognize.

"Set my glass on the island. I'll be right out." Her voice was hollow, absent.

I did as I was told, heading out to the back porch. But instead of settling into the porch swing, I leaned against the wall, listening. Fine, eavesdropping. Not common practice for me, but tonight was far from common.

"This is important to me, Gran. I want to lead the Lammas ritual. I need you to let me."

"All right, Evan. I didn't realize how important it was."

I heard him sigh. "Thanks, Gran."

I peeked in just in time to see him plant a kiss on her cheek. His eyes caught mine, but they weren't the baby blues that made girls in town swoon. They flashed dark as midnight.

And then the flash of darkness was gone, and he was Evan again.

"Sure, you don't want me to play for you, Gran? I've got my guitar in the truck."

She stared at him. "Evan, my darling, I think you'd best go home. Maybe throw some laundry in the wash so your mom has clean clothes. I suspect she'll have her hands full with bringing those twins into the world."

"Anything for my favorite ladies. Night." He blew her a kiss.

Halfway down the porch steps, he tilted his head back toward me. "Going into town later. You want to come?"

"No. I told Gran I'd repair the chicken coop first thing in the morning."

He laughed, the sound merry, blessedly normal. "Suit yourself, old man." He hopped in his rebuilt Mustang. "Suit yourself."

Then he fishtailed out of the driveway like he hadn't just magicked our grandmother.

Gran stepped out onto the porch and sat on the swing. "Sit down and drink your tea." She patted the seat beside her, rocking the swing with her bare feet against weathered wood.

The songs of night insects filled the air. "I know. Don't fret. I know. We can't stop the shadows. Not yet. I don't know why. The timing isn't right, the way you know a plant isn't ripe for harvesting. Live a life long enough, you know these things."

The swing creaked as we rocked back and forth.

She hummed.

I hummed along.

Cassie
Lammas, August 1, 2018

The night air was humid. A familiar buzz of energy hung in the air—in the din of chatter between sister and brother witches, in the magic of the basic tools of the coven, in the mixing and mingling of the witches' elemental energies.

I'd seen Nick's memory of the kitchen. I followed him in his journey, somehow knowing not much time had passed—a few days.

The coven members assembled at the banks of the creek. A low wooden table served as an altar, covered in new potatoes, crookneck squash, and a few red and green tomatoes. A circle of herbs surrounded the altar which included two wood-carved statues—the Green Man, lord of the forest, resplendent in his crown of antlers and leaves, and the Great Mother, her face serene, yet ancient and wise, her hands cupping a belly swollen with child.

With us. With the world. With nature. With magic.

I smiled.

A tall, curvy woman in a red broomstick skirt and black peasant top carried a wicker basket down the hill and set it beside the altar. She smiled and tucked a stray strand of blond hair behind her ear.

"All right, sisters, I've got the drums and shakers for tonight. Mama's bringing the Lammas loaf."

I couldn't help but stare. I saw Ginny's wisdom in her eyes. She was tall like her mother, with the same fair hair, but she had a magnetism, an earthy charm that was all her own, and I couldn't help but admire it.

She glanced in my direction, her brow furrowing. Her eyes were deep brown, her cheekbones high, her cheeks pink in the dying sunlight. She seemed to stare right at me, and I automatically stepped back, feeling like an interloper.

I shook my head. *Relax. She can't see you.*

"Maeve, I brought the honey mead for tonight," said a woman with pixie-cut, gray hair. She planted a kiss on Maeve's cheek. There was more than a bit of mischief in her dark eyes, hooded in a smattering of bright blue eyeshadow.

Tricia. Though her long black hair was faded to gray, she was unmistakable. She wore a long black dress with a silver belt, the silver bangles at her wrists jangling as she leaned forward to set the bottle on the altar. She must've been in her seventies now, but she sparkled just as fiercely as ever.

"How's your granddaughter?" the woman asked Tricia.

"Oh, Bailee's good. She's doing some short-term library work in Richmond for the public library system. I called her last night and tried to get her to come, but she was in the middle of, I don't know, cataloging something or the other." Tricia waved her hands dramatically as she spoke.

Another woman, in her thirties, stepped in, and Maeve enveloped her in a hug, and they started chatting about something that sounded like a series of books, but one I'd never heard of.

Ginny made her way down the hill—still perfectly Ginny, even after all these years. Her hair was in a silvery braid that draped over one shoulder. Her clothing, a brown and green patchwork skirt and brown t-shirt, was understated, but somehow just right for the occasion.

She smiled and waved. "Hi, sisters." But the smile didn't carry to her eyes, and she kept glancing at the sky, at the creek, at the darkening woods.

She set a loaf of bread on the altar, and Maeve arranged the candles and offerings around it. I studied Ginny, her expression dark and cautious as the sisters milled about, laughing and chatting and hugging. She smiled and talked when spoken to, but her mood seemed far too somber.

Of course, she knew. Ginny had a way of knowing. She always had.

Dusky shadows filled the forest, and the birdsong quieted. Ginny clapped her hands, but the din of chatter was already fading.

"Okay, everyone, Evan is up at the house getting ready. He's going to lead tonight, but he asked me to go ahead and call the quarters and cast the circle."

As she spoke, a quiet figure stepped into the circle. Nick. His hair was shorter, his beard more neatly trimmed, but it was my Nick. He accepted a few hugs and offered a few words and half-smiles before a sister stepped forward and the witches turned toward the East, asking the air elementals to bless the circle.

A wave of air magic swept over the circle, the candle flames flickering, and the soft, harp-like melody of sylph song drifted over the sacred space, blessing it before fading.

Another sister turned to the South and asked fire and the salamanders to bless the circle. They then faced West, toward Willow Creek, and were blessed with the high, lovely singing of the water undine.

They faced North. Ginny nodded pointedly at Nick, who stepped forward and cleared his throat, summoning the power of earth and the gnomes. His work done, he retreated into the waiting circle.

Lastly, they faced center, and summoned spirit.

The circle hummed with energy. Maeve took various types of hand drums—djembe, bongos, and even gourds filled with rice—out of the basket, and passed them around.

The circle was cast.

Now they'd draw down the energy. I ached for it, felt the electricity of it humming along my skin. Candle wax and bonfire. That's what a coven's magic smelled like.

The drumming, shaking, stomping, and chanting started out low, slowly building.

There was a wild, feral cry from the forest, and the drumming and chanting stopped. Everyone froze.

Nick's brother—scarcely recognizable from the vision I'd seen from a few nights prior—stepped into the circle with a dark grin.

His blond hair was pulled back into a sleek ponytail. Black makeup rimmed his eyes, making the blue seem somehow menacing, like a winter sky on a windy January day.

He tilted his head skyward and let loose another animalistic cry.

"Welcome to the circle, sisters." He spun to face Nick. "And brother." I didn't miss Nick's scowl. He didn't care for the theatrics, clearly. Neither did Ginny, from the looks of it. The other witches looked uneasy, too, and shifted in their places.

Evan held his palms skyward and raised them emphatically, like a rock star trying to pump up a crowd. "Come on now. Drum. Make music."

The drumming began again, but there was an uncertainty hanging in the air.

That Evan stood in the center was unusual. Even the high priest or priestess for the evening was expected to stand with the others around the circle—Ginny's way of reminding us that no one was above anyone else.

The drumming pounded, almost making my head ache though it usually set me at ease. I grit my teeth. Evan swayed to the music, clad in tight-fitting black pants and a black denim shirt. He paced the inside of the circle like a jungle cat, chanting low and deep, the words too quiet to hear.

The sky darkened fully into night. The drumming softened and then ceased, the magic buzzing so intensely my head throbbed. This was wrong. It felt so terribly off from the sweet excitement of the rituals I'd known.

Evan puffed himself up and withdrew something from his pocket, a small leather pouch.

He dumped the contents into his hand and sprinkled them onto the altar. "With this dirt, I consecrate this altar." He tugged something out of his back pocket. A pocket knife. It gleamed red in the candlelight.

He opened the knife and sliced his palm before anyone had time to react.

He made a fist, dripping blood onto the altar, staining the sacred loaf, causing candle flames to pop and sizzle.

"Evan, stop this!" Maeve rose, going to his side and tugging at his arm. "Sisters, I'm sorry. I don't know what's come over him." She grabbed his arm, trying to guide him away from the altar, but he shoved her hard enough that she stumbled back into the other sisters.

She glared. "Evan Matthew Felson, that's enough."

Evan laughed, the sound sinister. "Middle-naming me won't stop this, Mom. I was chosen."

"Chosen?" She quirked an eyebrow. "By whom?"

"Stop talking, and you'll see."

Tricia stepped forward. "You don't talk to your mother—or any woman—that way."

Evan sent her a deadly glare, but said nothing.

Nick started to step forward, but Ginny grabbed him, tugging him back in line with the other witches. She whispered something. He nodded, crossed him arms over his chest, and said nothing, just clenched his jaw.

Evan turned back to the altar.

"Dance in the shadows, sylphs. Swim in the inky depths, undine. Tunnel deep in the earth, gnomes. Salamanders, burn for the shadows. For now I call all of you to do the bidding of shadow."

He began to hum, something dark. "The shadow dwells here now." He blew out a candle, then another. "The shadow dwells here now." Witches tried to step forward to stop him, but some invisible hand seemed to stop them, a force pressing on them, keeping them away. One by one, he extinguished the candles.

Darkness fell. Evan let loose another feral cry.

Rain fell heavy. A roar filled the air. Thunder shook the forest so hard my head throbbed with it.

"Nick. We need blue kyanite. Hurry!"

And then I was following Nick, and he was running. I'd never seen anyone move so quickly, with such long strides. He fell in the dark forest, jumped up, kept going. Rain blurred my vision—and surely his.

Up the steps, into the house, straight to the closet. He tore through its contents, tossing random items aside until he found a wooden box. He dug within, and I couldn't help but notice how quickly he identified the kyanite, a sure sign of one of Ginny's students. He stuffed it into his pocket and ran back.

By the time he reached the top of the hill overlooking the creek, the wind was howling, banshee-like. Thunder shook the earth.

No. It wasn't just the wind. It was the shrieks of the sylphs and the undine, a horrific howl as someone tried to draw their energy away.

Whatever Evan had summoned—that creature, person, whatever or whoever it was—was stealing the energy, the magic of the elemental creatures of Willow Creek, syphoning it toward their own purposes.

"Gran! Mom!"

Ginny turned. "Stay there, Nicholas! I'll come to you." The wind almost tore the words away.

Nick started down the hill.

Evan turned, glaring. "No, brother. Not this time." He held out his hand and sent Nick flying.

Nick hit the ground hard. He rose with a grimace and started once more down the hill.

The creek was no mere trickle now, but the wave came out of nowhere. The screams would stay with me forever, the sheer terror.

The storm, the wind, the cries of witches and elementals alike had disappeared. An eerie quiet fell, but only for a moment.

Nick stood on the hill overlooking the creek. His scream was like nothing I'd ever heard.

Cassie
Present day

My eyes snapped open. We were still on the bathroom floor.

And Nick's scream, this time, wasn't a memory.

I held him, rocking him like a small child.

Not knowing what else to do, I hummed, and then choked words rose up in my throat.

"Where the undine sings her sweet, wild song,
I met my beloved there.
Where the willow drapes her green, green hair,
I met my beloved there.
Where water flows over tumbled stone,
Where magic meets the earth,
Where the willow drapes her green, green hair,
I met my beloved there."

It was off-key, but Nick's scream softened as I sang, and his eyes flickered open. He clung to me, and then we were rocking each other, like the two lone survivors of a shipwreck.

"I don't know why. I don't know why he did it, or why I couldn't stop him."

"It wasn't him."

Nick snapped his head back to study me. "What?"

"That wasn't your brother. Something—or someone—used him, took him over. Some sort of spell."

"Crap." Nick rubbed his temples in circles. "I should've seen."

I squeezed his arm. "No."

Nick's eyes widened. "That's what she meant. She said I had to go to the Crossroads and bring him back."

"Ginny told you this? To bring Evan back from the Crossroads? Like, the Crossroads of Magic, where the four elements meet?"

He nodded. He stood on obviously quivering legs and splashed water on his face repeatedly.

"You can barely stand, Nick."

He turned. "I have to save them."

I pressed his face, still burning despite the cold water dripping from his chin. "We will." I leaned forward. "I swear it."

"Tonight?"

"Sure." I wasn't sure what he wanted to do was possible, but he was right. The Willow Creek Coven members were trapped. We were the only ones who could do something about that. "At the witching hour?"

He furrowed his brow as if considering, then nodded. "Midnight works. I have…A friend of mine, a fellow witch. She might be willing to help us. It would be a big spell."

"I agree. In the meantime, why don't you go lie down? I'll make us something to eat and put together the supplies."

"Have you ever done this sort of thing?"

I shrugged. "Has anyone?"

"No one I know."

"We'll figure it out."

I guided him toward his bedroom and tucked him into bed with a kiss on his forehead. His hair was damp, and I smoothed it from his brow.

On my way out, I picked up the photograph of the oak tree, studying the contours that marked my face. I blinked, then hung it on the wall.

Family. You must untangle the past.

The voice came to me, clear as a bell.

I closed the door softly behind me. "Mine?" I asked, my stomach clenching. "Or his?"

Yours. The future is rooted in the past.

I couldn't. Not tonight. Maybe not ever. Untangle those roots, unbury that pain? Nathan would be in his late sixties now, and my parents pushing ninety, if they were still alive. But even now, forty-five years in the future, I was still afraid to face them.

"No."

And then I opened the refrigerator, trying, as I'd so often done, to busy myself with something useful, to find some way to ignore those gnawing, aching thoughts that threatened to bubble up.

CHAPTER TEN

Nick

The smell of frying butter and onions woke me. My stomach growled, reminding me of how little I'd eaten today. A glance at the clock told me we had a little while until Bailee arrived—a newfound witch friend in tow.

I splashed some cold water on my face in the bathroom and brushed my teeth, finger-combing my hair and trying to sweep the cobwebs of the dreamless sleep away.

A dread, heavy as a boulder, stuck in my gut, but for the first time in a long time, there was hope—and that was something.

In the kitchen, Cassie was dipping chicken in bread-crumbs.

"Can I help?"

She smiled. She'd put Gran's handsewn blue floral apron over the borrowed clothes, her hair tied back in a loose ponytail with a rubber band. She shook her head. "I'm good." She gestured to the table. "Sit."

I circled my neck. "I need coffee. It's going to be a long night."

"We broke your coffee thing."

"I think there's an old coffeemaker in the attic some-where. Gran always kept lots of extras up there. While I'm at it, I'll see if I can't find you something better to wear." I eyed her up and down, raising an eyebrow. "Not that you don't look fantastic in that."

She rolled her eyes, then shooed me away. "Go. I could use some coffee too."

"Do you want music?"

"Are you going to sing for me?"

"No. We're one of the few remaining towns that has a local, independent radio station. They play music live from the Thirsty Fiddler on Saturday nights."

"That would be great." With that, she plopped the breaded chicken breasts in a pan of oil, stepping back as the oil popped and sizzled. As I adjusted Gran's old radio, I spied green beans in butter with caramelized onions and potatoes boiling on the back burner.

The twang of a banjo sounded, and I adjusted the volume. Cassie was already tapping her foot in time to the music as I opened the door to the attic and climbed the narrow, rickety steps.

At the top I fished for the pull chain for the light. As a kid I'd hated this, fishing around in the dark for that chain, not sure what I'd see when the light finally came on.

I tugged the chain, and the bare bulb filled the attic with yellow light. Gran kept a lot of stuff, but she packed everything meticulously and had tried to keep everything neatly arranged. The downside was that she had her own organizational system, and knowledge of it had vanished with her.

I rummaged around, finding everything from an old tricycle covered in *Ninja Turtle* stickers to a threadbare old footstool I'm sure she'd planned on restoring to its former glory.

When I opened a box of mismatched dishes, I figured I was close. I hunted through more boxes, finally finding an old, burnt-orange coffeemaker. If we were lucky, it wouldn't catch fire when we turned it on. Worst case, I had the stovetop one, but I'd never mastered making coffee in it that didn't taste like battery acid.

As I went to leave, something caught my eye—a brown plaid suitcase, oversized, sitting beside the stairs. As though it were waiting.

I set the coffeemaker down and clicked open the latches on the suitcase. On top of the stack of neatly folded clothes there was a photo. On the back, in Gran's cursive scrawl, was written "Willow Creek Coven. Beltane. 1974."

And there, surrounded by the others, was Cassie.

Beneath the photo was an envelope with Cassie's name on it. It wasn't yellowed but instead fresh, as though it had been written yesterday.

I somehow managed to heft both the large suitcase and coffeepot downstairs. I carried the suitcase into the living room and stopped in the doorway to the kitchen. "There's something you should see."

Cassie looked up from the potatoes she was mashing with the handheld masher. "I'm almost done here."

While she finished the potatoes, I turned off the burners and covered the waiting food with lids. I turned down the radio, a local bluegrass band playing an Appalachian rendition of an Irish jig.

She wiped her hands on her apron, then untied it. She frowned at me. "Couldn't find the coffeemaker?"

"I found something for you." I tugged her hand and led her into the living room.

Her eyes widened when she saw the suitcase. "She kept it."

"Of course, she did. Gran kept everything." I nudged her forward, my hand a gentle coaxing at the small of her back. "Open it."

Cassie knelt on the floor beside the suitcase, unhooking the latches. "Oh." Her voice was a purr as she studied the photograph. She took up the envelope, but her gaze traveled to the clothes. "She kept all of my handmade clothes. Everything I made myself." Tears welled up in the corners of Cassie's eyes. "Goddess, Ginny. I miss you."

Cassie pressed the envelope to her chest. The tune on the radio turned from a lively jig to a slow, somber ballad. She carefully slid her finger under the seal and opened the letter.

Her voice was raw and raspy as she read. "Dear Cassie, I know the journey hasn't been easy for you. I hope what you find with Nicholas reminds you that you are where—and when—you were always meant to be. I'd tell you not to forget to keep moving forward, but Goddess knows, you've never had much trouble with that. You will need to face your past sooner or later, I suspect, but that's not for me to say. Here are a few mementoes I kept for you. I knew the moment you stepped off that bus you'd be a great high priestess. That honor may fall to you soon enough. Merry meet, and merry part, until we merry meet again."

Cassie pressed the cream-colored paper to her chest. "Until we merry meet again," she whispered.

She rose and wrapped her hands around my waist. My arms encircled her, my hands running up and down her back.

Against my chest, she murmured, "I'm ready. For whatever comes next. We can do this."

I kissed the top of her head.

Like Gran, Cassie drew strength from her faith in magic and the goddess.

I closed my eyes. Hints of magic wafted through the air—woodsmoke and candle wax, moss and lavender.

Sweet Goddess, let me learn. Let me be what they need.

⚜

Cassie

After dinner, Nick hopped in the shower and I went through the contents of the suitcase. Each dress, blouse, skirt, and pair of handsewn jeans smelled freshly laundered.

Somehow, she'd known.

I chose a yellow blouse, the ruffles of which had been damned near impossible to sew. I'd finally only finished it with Ginny's help. I grabbed a pair of jeans in soft denim. Most of the women in town seemed to be wearing jeans with tapered bottoms, but if we survived our journey to the Crossroads, I'd have plenty of time to learn about 2019 fashion trends. I dug around the bottom of the suitcase, hoping that Ginny had tucked a pair of shoes away.

My hand brushed against something made of satin. My magic felt the energy of the stone inside before my brain recognized it. I opened it, sliding the stone into my hand.

An obsidian pendulum. The volcanic rock shone in the lamplight. I slipped the chain over my head. The energy was a little unsettling, a sort of restless tugging, but I sensed I would need it in the journey ahead.

I dug around some more and finally found a pair of

plain, brown leather sandals. I slid them on, the leather soft and supple even after all these years. I wiggled my toes.

I caught Nick watching me with a grin on his face.

"What?"

"You look very…Cassie-like."

I eyed him, nothing but a towel wrapped around his waist. "You look like a piece of Halloween candy I can't wait to unwrap."

"Yeah?" His voice was deep and husky. He moved toward me. His skin was still hot from the shower and smelled like spicy soap. He'd trimmed down his beard but kept the slightest hint of stubble.

I kissed him, a moan rising in my throat as he returned the kiss.

He leaned down and whispered, his breath warm against my ear. "When this is over, I want to spend an entire weekend doing nothing but making love to you."

My legs buckled, but Nick caught me with those strong arms.

Someone knocked at the door.

I drew back to stare up at him. "Who's that?"

"Reinforcements, remember? An old friend. And she said she knew someone."

The knock sounded again.

"Can you grab that? I've got to get dressed."

I sighed and shut the suitcase, then smoothed my blouse and opened the front door.

I flipped on the porch light.

Two women about my age stood there. One, tall and willowy, with red hair. She wore tattered jeans and a rosy pink t-shirt knotted at the bottom. The other was short and curvy, clad in a black polka-dot halter-top dress that flared at the bottom. Her hair was raven black with magenta streaks and cut in a chin-length bob. A silver hoop dotted her nose, complementing the deep plum lipstick she wore. She flashed me a warm grin.

"You must be Cassie. I'm Bailee Dugan." She drew me into an embrace like we were old friends.

"Hi," I said as she squeezed me a little too tightly.

She released me and eyed me up and down. "This is Vivienne. She's new in town, like you."

I caught the taller woman staring at me with the most peculiar expression. I held out my hand. "Hi. I'm Cassie Gearhart."

"Hi." The word sounded froggy, as though I made her nervous, and she kept studying me.

I shook my head, clearing the fog. "I'm sorry. It's been a long day. Please, come in. Nick will be right out."

I guided them into the living room, latching the suitcase and lugging it into the hall just as Nick emerged in his standard attire—t-shirt and a pair of jeans.

Bailee smiled at Nick. "Twice in one day, Saint Nick. Are we getting the band back together?"

Nick shrugged, that shy, distant part of him taking over. I was quickly coming to realize that there were only a handful of people Nick felt truly comfortable around. And I couldn't believe how lucky I was to be one of them.

"We need…" Nick raked his hand through his still damp hair and turned toward the window where dusk was giving way to night.

"We're casting a spell," I said.

Bailee tapped her fingers together. "What kind of spell? How does it align with the current moon phase?" She glanced at Nick. "I wish you'd given me more details in your text. 'Can you come by tonight? Magical stuff' is kind of vague."

Nick didn't turn, but I saw his shoulders stiffen, felt the raw wave of pain course over him to the point my stomach hurt. "They're alive."

Bailee's already pale skin turned a sickly pallor. She stood, then sat down, crossing and uncrossing her legs. "Are you sure?"

He nodded. "I had a vision. Gran said they're not dead." He sat in a floral armchair, sliding his legs out in front of him.

"You saw Ginny?"

Vivienne leaned forward. "Your coven, you mean?" She glanced at Bailee. "Your Grams?"

Bailee nodded. "Goddess. I knew it would take a lot for you to send out some sort of magical SOS, but…" She leaned her head back against the sofa. "All this time I thought she was gone."

"We all did," Nick said, the words ragged with regret.

I caught Vivienne staring at me again—like I was the ghost, back from the dead.

I tilted my head. "Have we met?" Recognition flashed inside me. "Sorry. Again, long day. At the farmers' market. I was outside the café."

She nodded. "I recognized you from your photo. Well, I'm pretty sure it's you."

"Oh. You knew Ginny."

She shook her head. She reached into her bag, black with a pattern of red cabbage roses. She withdrew a wrinkled photograph, decades old and worn as though it had been held a thousand times. She gave it to me.

It was me. I was eighteen years old. I wore a long, navy-blue skirt and a white, handsewn blouse. My graduation outfit.

I sucked in a breath. "Where did you get this?"

"I found it in my grandfather's things after he died."

The room blurred in and out of focus. "Nathan Gearhart was your grandfather?"

She nodded. "He raised me. Died in a car accident when I was thirteen."

My hands shook. "And you came to Willow Creek?"

"After I aged out of the foster care system." She took the photo back, smoothed it, tucked it gently back into her bag. "You're her, aren't you? His sister, Cassie."

"I...Yes. I sort of...Well, let's just say there was magic involved."

She raised her eyebrows. "That would explain a lot."

"Did he..." I was afraid to finish that sentence.

"Talk about you? Occasionally, mostly when he was..." She closed her eyes, opened them. "I found a piece of paper in his stuff with your name and an address in Willow Creek written on it after he passed. And the photo. But when I got here a few months ago, no one knew who you were—except for one older guy, who swore he knew you back then, but heard you'd moved to California."

The edges of my vision blurred. I closed my eyes. "Nathan's dead. He had a...son? A daughter? Children?"

"A daughter—Ruthie. She died when I was two. I never met my dad. Granddad raised me until he passed."

"And my parents—your great-grandparents?"

She shook her head. "Great-Gran had Alzheimer's. Granddad's father passed before my mom was even born."

I stood, walked to the window. My stomach ached. The back of my throat burned, raw with the passage of all the time I'd missed.

"No, Nick," I heard Bailee whisper beyond me.

Vivienne came to my side. I stared up at her. She had a good seven inches on me, easy.

"It's not your fault. I understand why you had to leave. I would've left too if I could've. Granddad was not a happy person. I don't know about Great-Gran—she was in a nursing home most of the time I knew her."

"I missed so much." I blinked, trying to clear my vision. "Foster care?"

She nodded. "Well, given that you're somehow my age, I don't know that there's anything you could've done. And I'm here now. I'm okay." She smiled, her hand flying to her mouth. "You're my Great-Aunt Cassie. The Big Bad Witch." Her eyes lit up with a familiar mischief. "I thought you'd be taller."

CHAPTER ELEVEN

Nick

It was Bailee, ever the outspoken one, who cleared her throat. "Vi, I know you and Cassie have a lot of catching up to do." She glanced at me. "Time travel? For real?"

I shrugged. "Sort of. Apparently, the Guardian trapped Cassie in an oak tree in 1974."

Everyone stopped talking. Vivienne and Bailee sort of gawked at Cassie, who shrugged. "That's a story for another night. We have a journey to make." She leaned up and hugged Vivienne. "You and I have many cups of tea ahead of us."

I studied Vivienne, seeing glimpses of Cassie, though they looked so different initially. Vivienne seemed as reserved as I was, whereas Cassie didn't seem to have that problem. They had the same green eyes, though, and I suspected the same intensity. Cassie and Vivienne turned to us.

Cassie clasped her hands together. "Ready?"

I stood up, rubbing my hands on my jeans. "You

practice, Vivienne?"

She nodded. "Fire magic."

"Air magic," Cassie chimed in.

"And I'm bringing the water magic tonight," Bailee said. "We've got the elements covered tonight, baby."

I filled Bailee and Vivienne on the basics of the spell—advanced magicks, to say the least.

"What's the plan?" Bailee asked after I'd finished.

"You and Cassie go to this Crossroads place, Vi and I stay here and ground you in this plane? Because that's a journey fraught with more perils than returning the One Ring to Mordor."

Only Cassie seemed confused by the reference. Apparently, she wasn't a Tolkien fan? That was a movie for another night.

"Bailee's a librarian," I explained to Cassie. "Expect a lot of literary references."

Bailee tossed her hands up in the air. "Literary. Movie. TV. Viral meme. I do them all."

Cassie wrinkled her nose. "Viral what?"

"Enough, Bailee," I said.

"Sorry," she mouthed. "Are we doing this?"

I winced. I'd forgotten how intense Bailee was—like a roaring waterfall of extroversion, especially when it came to magical experimentation.

"Should we do a reading first?" Vi asked. "I brought my tarot cards."

Cassie nodded and glanced at me. "That might be wise." There was hope—and a touch of curiosity—in her voice.

"It couldn't hurt." Truth be told, I didn't know I'd ever be ready for this spell. Or for any spell. But more info couldn't hurt.

Bailee tapped her foot, clearly eager to get started.

Cassie wrapped her arm around her newfound great-niece. "Let's use the kitchen table."

Bailee and I hung back. "Go easy, okay," I whispered. "This is…"

She glared at me. "My Grams has been trapped on some other plane, enduring Goddess-knows-what, for almost a year. Excuse me if I'm impatient."

I exhaled. "We're going to bring them back."

Her gaze sharpened. "I just feel so guilty. I'm off distracting myself with finishing my degree, trying to move on, and she's, they're…"

"Me too. I almost…" I lowered my voice. "I almost sold this place, took a job somewhere else. Thank the goddess Cassie got here when she did."

"We're ready," Cassie said, interrupting before Bailee could react. "Vi's going to do a simple three-card spread."

We sat around the kitchen table, the taper candles in their brass holders flickering, the lights dim.

"Three cards," Vi said, her voice husky and raw. Magic tingled across my skin, warm like a cup of chai tea on a crisp autumn night. Her hand hovered over the deck, cut into three stacks. "First card, past."

She withdrew a card and flipped it over. "King of Swords."

Her hand reached toward the second stack. "Second card, present." She flipped the card and frowned. "Knight of Swords."

Her fingers extended toward the final stack of cards. "Third card, future." She paused, inhaling and exhaling before she flipped the final card.

I scarcely dared to breathe, craning to see the cards but trying not to crowd.

The figure on that card? Seeing it felt like a punch in

the gut.

"Death." The word left her lips in a whoosh.

We all sat silent.

"It's okay," Vi assured us. "It doesn't always mean literal death. In fact, more often than not, it only represents the end of a chapter—the end of one phase, the beginning of the next."

Cassie rubbed my shoulder. "She's right." She glanced at Vi. "What about the other cards?"

Vi shook her head. "I don't know. The King of Swords is a powerful man who works his own will, one not to be angered, the sort of man who wields power with pleasure. You don't want to get on his bad side. And the Knight of Swords?" She wrinkled her forehead as she traced the edges of the card depicting a man riding a horse, charging boldly into the battle before him. "He's reckless, wearing, ambitious, maybe a little conceited. But also effective."

Bailee laughed a quick, lilting laugh. "Sounds like Evan."

I could only nod. "It does." A glance at the clock told me we needed to get moving. "Let's go see if we can't find him."

We packed up the supplies, silent, except for the odd magical question, or the sound of someone rummaging through supplies looking for a certain herb, gemstone, essential oil, or candle. I made sure I still had the nephrite jade in my pocket. Its energy was cool and calming, with a gentle buzz to it. I noticed Cassie kept touching a pendant tucked under her shirt, but I didn't ask—I figured if I needed to know, she'd tell me.

It didn't matter to me if anyone spoke. I could hear nothing, save the sound of my own heart pounding in my ears.

No panic attacks. Not tonight.

So much depended on my ability to wield magic, to parse its mysteries, to take all those disparate threads Gran had shown me and weave them into something useful enough to save the ones I loved.

❇

Cassie

"Think we brought enough crystals?" I asked as we added another half dozen to the twenty or so already forming the sacred circle.

"Can't be too careful," Bailee said as she added some selenite to the mixture of black shungite, iridescent labradorite, and the glistening purple of amethyst. She snapped her fingers. "It's not quite done. Something's missing."

"I think we're good," Vi said. "Maybe we've gone a little overboard?"

"My intuition tells me something is missing." Bailee shook her head. "My intuition is never wrong."

Cassie shook her head. "You are a *lot* like your grandmother. Tricia is your grandmother, isn't she?"

"Yeah. And my dad says the same thing."

Nick tugged something out of his pocket. We'd encircled ourselves with battery-powered lanterns, strings of fairy lights, and a few torches to light the night. The stone in his palm was pale green. I felt its energy pulsing, pure and earthy, yet light and ethereal.

I stepped into the center of the circle and held out my hand. He handed me the stone.

I closed my eyes. Its energy was of the earth, where mine was of the air, but I felt roots sinking down deep. I smiled and opened my eyes. "Nick, it's the key." I met his eyes. "Somehow, you have the key."

I handed it back. "It's called nephrite jade. Gran gave

it to me, years ago. It was missing for years. I just found it again last night, actually. Well, it found me."

"Eureka," Bailee said, but her voice was soft.

No one spoke. The energy shifted, a slight, subtle feeling telling our communal witches' intuition: it was time.

I took Nick's hand, and he stepped over the ring of crystals into the center. We sat encircled in their energy, thousands of tiny vibrations coursing through our bodies. I sighed and sank into the earth. It was familiar, now that I remembered those decades in the oak.

I took Nick's hands in mine. "I believe—in us, in our magic. Have faith."

He nodded. He didn't speak—maybe he couldn't— but I read his conviction in his eyes. I felt his nerves as well as my own, but I also felt his certainty. We were doing this.

Nick took the piece of nephrite jade, cupped it in one palm, and we stacked our hands together, a gentle press of flesh, a promise of magic shared.

Vi sat outside the stones on my side. Bailee took the other side. It made sense, Vi and I having a blood connection, Bailee and Nick having worked magic together before.

Vi hummed. Bailee joined in, a soft melody akin to a lullaby.

My limbs went heavy. It wasn't that the earth beneath opened up, but that I grew roots, tunneling down into its depths. I tasted the rain, the fallen leaves, the ever-churning power of the earth.

I let myself go heavy, the magic coming easily as Vi and Bailee's melody and the crystals opened the path. I pictured what I'd seen in that brief visit to the Crossroads.

And then the ground did open up, and we tumbled.

Tumbled.

Down.

�֎

Nick

My body hit with a jarring thud.

I sat up, rubbing my head.

Around me, pale mists writhed like serpents made of dry ice. The earth beneath was hard and packed, dark brown. From the ceiling above hung strands of silvery-green moss and crystalline points in rainbow hues.

I breathed in, a sour stench hitting my nose, and I coughed.

Beside me, Cassie leaned forward. "It's the same, but different."

"You've been here before?"

"Once." She spoke softly, in the trance of memory. "The night Nathan came looking for me. When I called on the Guardian for help, she brought me here. I didn't realize what it was then." She closed her eyes. "There was a throne. She seemed like a giant to me, an immortal being of magic."

Cassie stood, brushing herself off, and I did the same. The hair at the back of my neck prickled, goosebumps erupting on my skin.

Yeah, it was cold here, but that wasn't it.

I peered into the misty shadows.

Cassie wrinkled her nose. "The smell is new, though. Back then it smelled like wild magic—like damp stone, moss, fresh blackberries, a hint of woodsmoke."

We stared into the dark. We were standing at a crossroads—literally. Roads forked out in four directions, a worn wooden sign with arrows pointing various directions. But the words on the sign were in a strange script I didn't recognize, indecipherable to me. I knelt before it, my fingers brushing the silver lettering. "Gran was right, then. Some sort of shadow magic is coming for Willow Creek."

"For the elementals of Willow Creek. That's why, whatever it is, it needed the coven members out of the way."

I glanced up at her, grimacing. "Why did I survive, then?"

She cupped my cheek. "I don't know. Maybe for this, right here. So you—we—could save them." She reached for my hand and tugged me to my feet. "Come on. We don't know how long the magic will last."

"Which way do we go?"

"I knew this would come in handy." She tugged something out from under her shirt—a long, silvery chain, on which hung a black, shimmering stone. She unclasped the necklace and dangled it in front of her. "Obsidian to show the way."

"Clever."

"Don't be too impressed. Ginny packed it away in the suitcase."

There was a sound of something scurrying. Both our gazes darted in every direction, but the low, creeping mists shrouded anything below our ankles in mystery.

If that wasn't unsettling, I didn't know what was.

"Let's get moving," I said.

"Agreed," she said, the word rushed.

She held out the pendulum, waiting for it to still completely. "Guide us, Great Goddess. Show us the way."

We both stared at the pendulum. The seconds ticked by and then an unseen force tugged on it, urging us to take the path straight ahead.

I didn't speak, not wanting to break the spell. I cupped the nephrite jade in my pocket—the key to getting us into the Crossroads. And, who knew? Maybe the key to getting us safely out.

We crept along. The pendulum led us in an impossible series of twists and turns. There would be no navigating our way back to our starting point by memory—only magic.

The air around us hung heavy now with the stink of something foul. I recognized it as something strongly sulfuric, mixed with a heavy stench of mushrooms, and something musky. Unpleasant would be an understatement.

Rather, unsettling—because it represented a dark, sickening sort of magic I'd never known.

Magic is love—love of people, love of the earth, love of the goddess and god, love of the elements. Gran's words.

This was not the magic I'd been taught.

I covered my mouth. Cassie's face was a sickly gray in the dim light of the Crossroads, but she pushed on, her focus on the pendulum guiding us deeper into the labyrinthine underground.

There was a spellbinding sort of beauty to it, like the forest after an ice storm. Crystals and moss dangling above. Emerald green vines occasionally dangled, covered in roses the deepest of reds. Black boulders that seemed speckled with stardust occasionally jutted through the fog.

Something ancient, something powerful slept here.

All magic sleeps here, Nicholas. This place is magic, waiting to be born. I jumped at the sound of the raspy voice in my head. A woman's voice, lyrical yet pained.

Cassie stopped. "What?"

"Did you know, Cassie, what this place is?"

She glanced around us. "Sleeping magic."

"It's incredible."

"Beyond words," I whispered.

We pushed on. The stink of sulfur grew stronger, mixed

with a scent of dragon's blood incense and candle wax.

Not the scents of magic. Actual candle wax.

A wall of silvery mist swirled in front of us. Beyond it lay shadow, impenetrable.

We stared at the pendulum, waiting for answers. None came.

"What now?" I whispered, but the mists seemed to swallow my question.

Cassie shook her head and tucked the pendulum into her pocket.

"We go on faith."

"Faith in what?"

She took my hand. "In *our* magic, in our connection to it."

Was that my heart, thudding against my ribcage, or had I swallowed a hammer at some point?

"I don't..."

She unclasped my hand and pressed my other hand more firmly around the small green gemstone in my hand. "You do."

I squeezed the stone in one hand, Cassie's hand in the other. I sensed her fear like it was my own, but her resolve resonated even more strongly.

We stepped, hand in hand, into the mist.

CHAPTER TWELVE

Cassie

The white mist swirled around us. It smelled damp and cloying, but not unpleasant. At least in the fog we couldn't smell the sulfuric stink of whatever shadowy magic tainted this sacred underworld.

Sacred. That was the word for it. I could feel the ancient magic vibrating deep inside my core, my spirit responding. I felt it, its energy, and yet…it was dulled, asleep.

Oh, some spell had been cast. And the pendulum, as it had tugged me in this direction, seemed aware. I couldn't shake that feeling.

Tug.

Doom.

Tug.

'What lies ahead?' you ask.

Tug.

Darkness, dear witch. Darkness, wretched and deep.

Tug.

Even now it was heavy and ice cold in the pocket of my jeans where I'd tucked it. My heart, too, ached with the knowing that I shouldn't go on and yet that I—we—must.

Nick's hand was clammy against mine. We pressed on through the mist, unable to see. We tiptoed ahead, skirting the occasional rock or ducking the random dangling vine.

I gasped as a thorn scraped my skin.

"You okay?" Though Nick stood right next to me, the density of the fog distorted the sound, making him sound distant.

"I'm fine. Let's keep going."

The fog grew patchier, not enough to see far ahead, but at least I could see Nick's face again.

The tension in my gut, however, didn't ease.

Something began to pulse, like a great, giant drum, the vibration of which I could feel inside me. From the twisted grimace on Nick's face, I'd say he could feel it too.

The mists parted. Before us was the entrance to a massive cavern. The rock was dark, volcanic, like pumice, but glittering with flecks of gold and silver.

Nick's lips curled up. He released my hand and wiped both of his on his jeans. "Beyond this place, there be dragons."

"We can only hope."

I swallowed, fighting the bile that rose in my throat. Even as a kid, when magic was forbidden, I'd never feared it. I'd always yearned for it, the way a thirsty tree yearns for rain during a drought.

I'd known fear before, but fear of magic? Never. Definitely new territory.

I stepped forward, but Nick grabbed my arm, stilling me.

"I know Gran and Mom taught me ladies first, but I think we'll have to make an exception in this case, if that's okay with you."

I stared at the black maw of the cavern. "You haven't practiced magic in almost a year," I pointed out.

He sighed. "You're right." He glanced down at me. "I have to stop letting fear cut me off from my magic. Now."

With that, he stepped into the entrance of the cave. He was immediately plunged into darkness, as though a cloak of shadow had fallen over him.

"Nick? Nick!"

Nothing greeted me, save the eerie echo of my own voice.

Steeling myself, I stepped into the darkness. I blinked, my eyes adjusting to the strange light of the cavern. Torches flared in metal brackets on the walls, their flames several feet high. A high ceiling vaulted over us, black and speckled with quartz in many hues.

At the far end of the room stood a familiar sight—a throne seemingly sculpted of a living, sentient tree, its wood a deep, almost copper orange streaked with dark brown and dotted with vibrant pieces of peridot. Behind it, twisting, dark green vines climbed the cavern wall, dotted with large, ruby-hued roses. An underground stream waterfalled down another wall, flowing into a small pool of crystalline water. The scent of incense hung heavy in the air—enough that I almost gagged on it.

And then a wave of stench hit us, and both Nick and I stumbled back.

Sulfur. This place of beauty was being slowly poisoned.

There was a metallic rattle from a distant corner of the massive cavern, and a figure stumbled toward us.

His hands were shackled in black iron, his hair matted. His skin was bruised and bloodied.

He collapsed in front of us, staring at us with large, frightened eyes sunk deep within a hollow face. But I recognized those vivid blue eyes.

Nick fell to his knees. "Evan. Evan?"

The man stared, seeming disoriented. He tilted his head and reached out with his shackled hands. "Saint Nick?"

"Yeah." There was relief tinged with sorrow in that single word. "We're going home, baby brother."

Evan staggered to his feet, stumbling backward. "No. No! He'll kill us. He'll kill you for coming here. Goddess." He howled, the sound pure agony. "Goddess!"

Nick stepped toward his brother, but Evan flung his arms in front of his face in a defensive gesture.

I came to Nick's side. "He's clearly been through a lot. Let me try talking to him."

Slowly, Nick nodded, but his face remained twisted in that pained expression.

I took a single step forward, keeping my arms low. "Evan, my name is Cassie. I'm a friend of your grandmother's. We have a way to get you home."

Evan met my eyes. My heart nearly broke. His suffering was so raw, so apparent. "He will kill us all." He gestured toward the entrance of the cavern. "Go, before he gets here."

"Before who gets here?"

"Me."

Evan cried out and crashed to his knees. A figure, clad ironically in white, stepped forward. He had dark brown hair and a dark, neatly trimmed beard. But when his eyes met mine, I knew, even before he spoke, who he was.

He flashed me a menacing grin before turning to Nick.

He extended his arms in a falsely welcoming gesture. "Nicholas, we meet again."

Nick stepped backward. "Go to hell, Dad."

The man tossed his head back with a hearty chuckle.

"Nicholas, you know witches don't believe in hell." He eyed me and flashed impossibly white teeth. "But I'm trying to make the Crossroads and Willow Creek the closest thing possible."

�֎

Nick

Evan whimpered. My stomach heaved, but somehow, I kept its contents down.

Here I'd thought my dad was a royal bastard because he'd walked out on his wife and two kids.

But this? Never crossed my mind.

I stepped between him and Cassie.

I swallowed hard, biting back the angry words, the obscenities I'd sworn I'd hurl in his direction like Zeus's lightning bolts if I ever saw his face again.

My last memories were of a blue sports car that he'd tinker with on the weekends while Evan and I played with toy cars in the grass nearby; that same car, driving away, taillights disappearing; Mom's forced cheer as she announced we'd all go stay at Gran's for the night; the sound of her sobs after she thought we were asleep.

The sound of Evan's.

The pain of the tears I'd forbidden myself from shedding that night—and all the nights that followed.

Dad approached me. He tapped his forehead. "What's going on, son? You always were the thinker in the family. Got that from your grandmother, I reckon."

Cassie's eyes were wide. She hadn't looked this frightened before, not even in the kitchen when I told her that she'd traveled forty-five years into the future and her entire coven was gone.

Gone was the man who'd played fiddle while Mom and Evan danced and I hummed along. Gone was the man who let me sit atop his shoulders so I could see the Fourth of July parade floats go by, and the man who'd bought my brother his first guitar at a local pawn shop.

Now he was just a monster.

He placed a hand on Evan's shoulder, and Evan cowered.

"Don't touch him," I growled.

Dad smirked, but he let Evan go, held up his hands in a surrender gesture, and backed away. "As you wish."

"I'm taking Evan and leaving."

"Hmm." He cocked his head, as if we were negotiating the price of a used car. "Sure. Evan and I have come to an understanding."

Evan met my eyes. He shook his head. I knelt down, smoothed his matted hair away from his face. "It's going to be all right. We're going home now. To the farm. You'll be safe there."

He stared up at Cassie and shook his head.

I followed the direction of his gaze. Cassie had gone as white as new snow, one hand clasped over her left arm.

I rose. "What is it?" I pried her hand off her arm. Near the top of her left arm, just below the ruffle of her blouse, was a scratch.

"I cut myself on a thorn." That simple explanation didn't explain why her voice had gone flat, all emotion drained from someone usually so animated.

"We'll clean it up when we get back."

She shook her head.

Dad chuckled again. The hairs on my neck rose. I turned to see him holding something small and dark between his fingers—a single, emerald green thorn.

"I have her blood, Nicholas." His lips curled up. "It sings with her love for you. Precious. You've made your trade. Your lover for your brother. Now take him and go before I change my mind."

"No."

"You're trying my patience."

"I don't care." I lunged forward, determined to grab the thorn out of his hands, but he easily sidestepped me, and I crashed onto the rough, cold rock, my palms stinging.

He glared. "Go home. *Now*."

My vision blurred. An unseen force tugged on me, and I felt my body tugged upwards, back toward Willow Creek.

I couldn't leave her. I couldn't leave Cassie.

"Gran, help me! What do I do?"

I tried to hold myself in that strange, sickening, once-mystical place.

I can't leave her.

I can't leave her.

Evan clung to me, his grasp desperate, his whimper filling my ears.

I closed my eyes.

Gran, Gran, Gran.

I'm not Beetlejuice, Nicholas. Her voice swept over me, always calm, ever reassuring.

I can't leave her here.

I know. A tiny piece of home, a connection to you will guide her back. Soon, my love.

And then I felt her slip away.

The tug grew stronger. I could feel Bailee's presence, like a dewy field, urging me back to the banks of Willow Creek.

The nephrite jade sang in my pocket, reminding me of the sweet earth I'd tended all my life, a gift from my Gran to guide me in times of trouble.

With one hand, I tugged Evan to his feet. With the other, I pulled the jade from my pocket and tucked it into Cassie's hand.

"Remember who you are. Remember that I love you. I love you."

"I love you too."

But her voice was already fading.

And then I was blinking on the banks of Willow Creek, the first rays of sunrise tickling my eyes.

"No." I rolled onto my side. "No."

I glanced around, my body still inside the circle of crystals. Bailee sat there, and so did Vi. Evan was curled beside me, arms wrapped around his knees.

But Cassie?

She wasn't there.

CHAPTER THIRTEEN

Cassie

Nick and Evan vanished from sight. My breath came in ragged gasps, but I fought to stay focused.

"You remind me of someone."

Nick's father pressed the thorn between his thumb and forefinger. "Is that so?" His tone suggested disinterest, but I pressed on.

"Mm-hmm. My brother. He was just like you—drunk with power."

He flashed a dagger-like glance in my direction. "Your brother, my dear, *was* a drunk. He was drunk when he died in that car accident."

I stepped backward. "How do you know that?"

He shrugged. "I've been studying you and your family for a long time. I even know about the girl—Vivienne. Vi, they call her. Sleeping magic, that one."

My chest hurt. Sweet Goddess.

"Why do you care so much?"

He shrugged. "Girl gets trapped in an oak tree, guy gets curious."

I glared. "How would you know about that?"

"Maeve. She was a talker. Not like her mother. Not like Nick. She never sensed my magic. Some of us, you see, can cloak our magic. It's a gift. I have it." He shot me a look. "Your brother had it."

"My brother was not a witch." I gritted my teeth. "He hated magic."

"Hated it? Yes. Possessed it? Also, yes. Fire, like sweet, young Vi. It twisted and writhed inside him, unable to escape. Made him angry; made him mean. We're meant to embrace our true selves. Something you and I can both agree on."

"The high self is spirit, and the spirit is pure."

"Where'd you pick that line up? Miss Ginny's School of Witchery?"

I clenched my fists. The nephrite jade tingled in my palm, cool, though my hands were full of fire. "Actually, yes. She knew more about magic than you ever will."

Laughter sounded in my head. *Very true, Miss Cassie.*

Ginny?

The more he angers you, the stronger the bond. Focus on the ones you love. Let the jade guide you home.

Her voice was like aloe smoothed onto a bad sunburn. I bowed my head. "I'm sorry. Please explain."

His eyes narrowed. "Not likely. What are you up to?" He strode over to me and grabbed my wrist.

I winced in pain, but I held tighter to the stone. "Why? Why would you do this to magic? To your children? To your family?"

He leaned in, his face close to my ear, and I tried not to cringe. "That's not your story to hear."

I shivered, all the warmth going out of me.

I clutched the stone, remembering the feel of Nick's hands on my skin, the feel of his kiss. The scent of patchouli soap. The sight of that yellow farmhouse, how it always set my heart at ease. Chatting with Ginny while we stitched in the winter evening. The last swig of iced tea in the glass. The creak of the back-porch swing…

Nick.

I held onto the stone.

His anguish called to me, a desperate sort of beacon. Love. That's what it was. We'd only just begun to understand it, to explore it. His earth, my air. It drew me upward.

My body grew lighter. The jade vibrated with cool, earthy energy, sending tingles throughout my body, drawing me toward home.

And that's what Willow Creek and the Saunders Family Farm were to me—they were home.

And so was Nick.

"We're not done, girly," Nick's father taunted, but I was already soaring away.

I blinked. I wasn't next to the creek. I sat up, leaves brushing my face. Beside me rested the body of a once-great oak, now singed from a lightning strike.

I stood on shaky feet.

The jade lay beside me, a bright spot of green on the dark earth.

I heard Nick, at the banks of the creek, crying out, calling my name.

"Nick! I'm here!"

I shoved the stone in my pocket and started running. There was no clear path to the creek from the grove where I'd cast that spell summoning the Guardian all those years ago, though.

It seemed to take an eternity before I found a place to scurry down an embankment and walk the banks of the creek toward the ritual site.

Nick met me halfway.

And then I was in his arms, and he spun me in a circle. "Goddess, Cassie."

"Too tight. You're squeezing me too tight."

He set me down with a sheepish look, and I hugged my ribs. "Sorry. I thought you were gone."

"How long?"

"We were down there all night, it seems. I've been waiting at the creek bank an hour for you, calling you, hoping you'd somehow hear me and make it back."

"I did." I hugged him. "I did." I leaned back. The early morning sun was rising on a cool, clear day. Birdsong filled the air, and the creek sang its babbling song beside us. "And Evan?"

Nick's face darkened. "He's back at the farmhouse with Bailee and Vi…but he's not himself."

"Of course, he's not. But he will be. He's strong. I know it. We have to patient, that's all."

He bobbed his head, the gesture slow and uncertain. "I hope so."

He stared at the creek, his jaw set in a firm line.

"We have hope now. We can't let that go." I tugged his hand. "Let's go home."

His eyes widened. "I have to call Mary Jo."

"Who?"

"The realtor."

"Why did you…" I planted my hands on my hips. "You weren't going to—"

"I was hurting. And desperate."

"And now?"

"Now, I have a shot at a future. With the ones I love. With magic." His Adam's apple bobbed. "With you."

I took his hand, and he led us toward an easier path back to the main one leading to the farmhouse, toward the ones that waited for us.

This was it. A new beginning. A fresh start. There was no going back to 1974.

It didn't matter.

I suspected everything I'd ever wanted had been waiting for me, in this time, in this place, with this man, all along.

Acknowledgments

I honestly don't know where to start! So many people have helped, supported, and encouraged me on the journey to writing this book.

First, I have to thank my husband, Ryan. Thank you, Ryan, for nearly two decades of love, laughter, and gratuitous Stargate references. Whether we're binge-watching Buffy, dreaming about buying a house in the country, or trying to navigate a foreign country, all our time together means so much to me. Thanks for believing in me, for being the best first reader a girl could ask for, and for making me laugh.

I have to thank all of the wonderful people who've made this book possible: to Amelia and Katie, who've been with me since the beginning. You're both the best critique partners I've ever had, and there's no one with whom I'd rather spend an afternoon eating spinach dip and talking Enneagram. To Victoria Cooper, graphic designer extraordinaire; editor Susan Bischoff of The Forge Book Finishing; and the team at Maple Cat Press, thank you for the hard work you put into helping me make *Tangled Roots* ready for its debut. Thanks, also, to Sarra Cannon, whose words of wisdom, advice, and inspiration gave me the courage to make my dream of being a published author a reality.

For Ems, my bestie, for twenty-plus years of friendship, mischief, and adventure. Where would I be without you?!

Special thanks to my mom, who taught me to love books, and my dad, who taught me to dream big and work hard. And to my brothers, for just being so awesome. No one will ever make me laugh as hard as the two of you.

And I can't finish these acknowledgements without thanking the awesome community at A Round of Words in 80 Days, for so many years of support and encouragement.

ROW80 truly is the kindest, most compassionate group of writers I've ever known. Thank you all so much! And thanks, Shan and Eden, for keeping the community going strong!

And many thanks to Gina Briganti, amazing friend, talented writer, and beautiful soul. Here's to many more sunny days at Coastal Magic Con!

About the Author

Equal parts bookworm, flower child, and eclectic witch, Denise D. Young writes fantasy and paranormal romance featuring witches, magic, faeries, and the occasional shifter.

Whatever the flavor of the magic, it's always served with a brisk cup of tea–and the promise of romance varying from sweet to sensual.

She lives with her husband and their animals in the mountains of Virginia, where small towns and tall trees inspire her stories. She reads tarot cards, collects crystals, gazes at stars, and believes magic is the answer (no matter what the question was).

If you've ever hoped to find a book of spells in a dusty attic, if you suspect every misty forest contains a hidden portal to another realm, or if you don't mind a little darkness before your happily-ever-after, her books might be just the thing you've been waiting for.

Visit Denise at www.denisedyoungbooks.com, where you can also sign up for her author newsletter, or join her on Facebook, Instagram, Pinterest, Twitter, or Goodreads.